Bound to Him

Bound to Him

DELILAH FAWKES

DEDICATION

Dedicated to the love of my life, my partner in crime, and to everyone who aims to misbehave.

Chapter One

"I have a present for you, little slave."

Mr. Drake sat in his study, a burgundy robe making him look regal, even over his silk pajama pants. A fire roared next to him, casting him in flickering shadows, but the intensity of his gaze was hard to miss.

I still couldn't believe he was mine, and I was his. What a wonderful life I led, and to think all of it started when I became his personal assistant just a year ago.

I knelt before him, my hands bound behind me with leather cuffs, waiting for his instructions, clad only in a barely-there red bra and panties, and the black garter and stockings he'd requested I wear.

"Would you like to see it?" He reached down and tilted my chin up, his lips twitching into a smirk. "You may speak, Mrs. Drake."

I smiled before answering. "Yes, please, Sir."

He chuckled, his long fingers stroking my cheek. "Good girl. Come with me."

He hooked a finger through the O-ring at the front of my collar, steadying me as I rose to my feet. The secret door to his dungeon… *our* dungeon… slid open, and he covered my eyes from behind. As the door slid shut and closed with a solid thud, I felt his lips on my neck and shivered, my body already humming with anticipation. What did this man wanted to give me? What did he have in store?

He took his hands away, and whispered, "Open your eyes."

His breath was warm on my ear, his body so close I could feel his heat, but he resisted touching me, waiting for me to look at what he'd prepared for us first. I did as I was told, and gasped aloud.

Before me was what looked like a burgundy leather-covered half-circle, supported on four, sturdy, black wooden legs. It looked like a bloody sunrise over a dark landscape. I couldn't help but notice the wrist and ankle restraints on each of the four corners. On top of the curve sat a golden bow. I grinned.

My own personal Santa Claus. Or should it be Santa Claws? I wondered if I'd be stretched over it face-first with my ass in the air, or if he'd be bowing my back over it… The latter thought filled me with a chilling foreboding that made fear prick my heart and my core heat with wonder.

What was Mr. Drake going to do to me on that thing?

"Do you like it, slave?"

I turned just enough to look at him. "I… I'm not sure, Sir. What it is for?"

Mr. Drake grinned at me in a way that made me want to squirm, but I held my body still, waiting eagerly for what he had in store for me.

"So many things, my dear Isa… whatever I'd like." He caressed my throat with one hand, making me shiver at his touch. "Today, I'd like you to lie on your back. Do you trust me?"

I nodded, looking at the device. I would be totally spread out for him. Totally vulnerable. My stomach did a little flip at the thought.

"Yes, Sir."

"Then go lie down, my beautiful little slave," he whispered in my ear.

I did as I was told, moving carefully to position myself on the half-circle, my back arching awkwardly as I lay on top of it. I tried to relax, and felt my body easing into the new position, my toes pointed toward the floor. I raised my arms above my head, and felt Mr. Drake's strong grip as he held my wrists. He bound first one and then the other, tightening the buckles on the restraints so I couldn't move, but was comfortably held in place.

He ran his hands down my body slowly in the dim light of the dungeon, caressing the tips of my breasts through my lingerie then whispering his fingers over my quivering belly, before lightly grazing my sex through the lace. I whimpered, my nerves already on fire for him, alert and ready for whatever he had in store.

He ran his hands down the inside of my thigh, and I tried not to moan, biting my lip as he moved lower, his touch agonizing in those ticklish areas, but strong. Sensual. When he secured my ankles, I felt the tension leaving my body, felt myself draping over this odd piece of furniture, my mind submitting to him as well as my flesh. It felt so good to let go—to trust him with every part of me.

That was what was so astounding about Mr. Drake. The trust I had in him, and him in me. That was my bliss.

I heard a scratching noise, then a faint hiss in the darkness of the dungeon's shadows, then smelled sulfur and saw the flickering light of a match. He lit a fat, black candle, and as he brought it closer, I could smell the scent of melting wax.

I tensed, then, not knowing what to expect. Mr. Drake had never used fire before, and although I trusted him with my life, a knife's edge of fear sliced through me. I whimpered as he drew closer.

"Shhh, little slave. Stay quiet, or I'll be forced to *really* punish you."

I pressed my lips together, my eyes growing wide as he held the candle over me. He tilted it, and a single drop fell, spattering my exposed cleavage with hot wax. I wanted to scream, although the sensation was not altogether unpleasant. It was like stepping into a bath that was too hot, scalding, but that you knew you could stand if you had the nerve.

A thrill echoed inside of me, the rest of my body deliciously cool in comparison, my nerves suddenly alert and thrumming. I watched the candle bob above me in my master's teasing hands, and realized I was tensing all of my muscles, arching against the restraints, anticipating the next drip.

"Something's not quite right," he said, his voice low, his eyes full of hunger.

I heard a metallic scraping, like a steel instrument being taken off an aluminum tray. Then, I saw the flash of scissors, and bit down a whimper as they slid beneath the band of my bra, the sharp metal nestled between my breasts. A loud *snickt*, and the lace fell away, leaving me bared to the wax.

My nipples pebbled in the cool air, and I squirmed, trying to catch a glimpse of Mr. Drake, who'd moved into the shadows again. My field of vision was narrow, bent over almost backwards like I was, and I trembled, not knowing if he was coming at me from above or what else he had in store.

I felt something cold creep under my panty line and swallowed a gasp. Another *snickt, snickt*, and I felt the cool air of the dungeon hit my exposed pussy. I was already so wet for him, so ready. I knew my thighs were glistening with arousal.

A drop of hot wax hit my stomach and trickled downward. I let a hiss out between my teeth as the sensation washed over me. I felt it hardening on my skin, and shivered. Another drop, higher, hit the apex of my curved body and rolled toward my breasts before drying, seeming to sizzle on my flesh all the way.

The sting and heat were mixing together into an aching pleasure so intense I wanted to scream. I wanted my husband inside of me. Wanted him to grab my hips and thrust inside of me, but I knew this delicious torture was turning him on as much as it was me. I knew, watching me from the shadows, seeing my body arch and writhe, watching my face the moment the wax hit, was making him rock hard. Making him as wild as I felt, if not more so.

A trickle of wax hit my nipple then, and I did scream, the sensitive nub on fire. The other was covered in wax as Mr. Drake leaned over me, grinning like the devil. I pulled against my restraints gasping, no longer caring if I made too much noise, unable to help myself as he moved his hand lower…

When the hot wax hit my lower lips, dripping down and hardening on my clit, my wail filled the dungeon, echoing off the walls and back into my ears. I shook my head from side to side, the sting overwhelming my senses, while I was so sensitive, so close to cumming, I thought I might die if I didn't have him inside me soon.

"You're going to get it now, little slave," he growled.

His hand came down on first one breast, then the other, slapping the stinging flesh until I howled again, my core aching for him, aching to be filled as the sensations flowed into me—through me.

I felt him pulled at the restraint beneath one ankle, then felt the leather strap part from the buckle. He grabbed my leg, pushing my thigh upward, spreading me open, even while I was still helpless, strapped down to the table by three points. There was nothing I could do to resist him as he pushed himself up on one knee, mounting the curved space between my thighs.

"I'm going to have to punish you well. Since you seem to love making noise against my wishes, I'm going to make you scream until your fucking throat feels like sandpaper."

I moaned, knowing he would make good on his promise.

He was shirtless now, his body gleaming with beads of sweat, and although I couldn't raise my head very far, I knew he held himself ready, stroking his long shaft as he positioned himself at my entrance.

I screamed as he sheathed himself inside of me in one stroke, up the hilt in one sure thrust. He pinched my nipples, and I felt the wax cracking on my sensitive flesh as he began pistoning, moving inside of me so hard and fast, I arched again, pulling against the bonds holding me, but this time wanting to hold him, to urge him on, to grab his ass and dig my nails into his skin as he fucked me again and again.

My body was on fire, my skin alight, although the candle had fallen forgotten to the floor long ago. Mr. Drake mercilessly thrust into me, pressing my thigh back until my knee met my shoulder. I felt him so deep inside of me, I pulsed around him, my pleasure ratcheting up until I was crying out like an animal.

He leaned down, biting at my breasts, and I moaned again and again, gasping as he suckled one into his mouth, even as he thrust inside me again and again. My body tensed, and then I was coming apart, my body shaking as I wailed, my core convulsing around him as he fucked me, driving into me harder and harder as I bucked up to meet him.

When he came, he gripped me tight, pulling my hips down to meet him, grunting as he spilled himself inside of me. He held me like that for a long while, his eyes closed in ecstasy, before leaning over me and kissing me long and deep.

He rubbed my wrists after he undid my bonds, nipping me lightly on my bottom lip.

"My throat isn't sore yet, Sir," I said.

He laughed, and swatted me on the breast again.

"Then we're just going to have try harder next time."

"I hope you remember," Mr. Drake said as he ran the washcloth lovingly over my breasts, soaping me and teasing me, "That we're having company tonight."

"Mmm," was all I could manage as I leaned back against his hard chest.

I did remember. One of Mr. Drake's friends was coming over for dinner and drinks. Apparently they hadn't seen one another in a couple of years, but had kept in touch.

"We used to be members of the same club," he said.

He kissed along my neck, tasting the rivulets of water cascading down my skin.

"I think you would have enjoyed it. It was a BDSM club. Very exclusive."

That got my attention. A whole club full of people like my Mr. Drake?

"It was a club for only the wealthiest clients, which meant only the best of everything."

He sighed and turned me around to face him. I slid my arms around his neck and met his serious gaze.

"Maxwell's father owns an auto empire, so he and I met in prep school. As we grew older, we quickly found out we shared certain tastes... and well, the rest is history. It will be good to see him again after so long. I'd invited him to our wedding, but he was out of the country on business."

I leaned in and kissed my husband, still blown away by the fact that he was mine, and I was his—that this was reality, living with him, loving with him, sharing his life.

"If he's anything like you, then I can't wait to meet him."

* * *

The doorbell rang as I was putting on the diamond earrings Mr. Drake gave me for my birthday. I glanced at the clock, confused. It was still an hour before Maxwell Pierce was scheduled to arrive.

I snuck to the edge of the bannister and listened, wondering why our guest would be so unfashionably early. I heard our butler, Mr. Daniels, speaking in soft tones, but instead of the masculine voice I'd expected, I heard a young woman's frantic explanations.

"Please! I need to see Isa… I mean, Mrs. Drake, right away. It's urgent!"

I froze at the top of the stairs. I recognized that voice as well as I recognized my own. My hand flew to my mouth, and I rushed down the stairs and across the foyer. Standing in the doorway, her red hair frizzy from the misting rain outside, stood my sister. My baby sister, Lucy, tears staining her cheeks.

"Thank you, Mr. Daniels," I said, putting my hand on the silver-haired man's shoulder. "I've got it from here."

When I turned back to my sister, I simply opened my arms and let her rush into them. I held her tight, letting her cry, stroking her hair and feeling a mixture of joy and sadness wash over me. She was here, in my new home, finally here with me, after so many months of being apart. She'd finally managed to get away, like she said she would.

But this wasn't a happy visit, was it? It couldn't be. Here she was, shivering in my arms, clutching my back like a woman drowning. What had happened to my sweet sister? And who was watching our rambunctious brother Alex, keeping him out of trouble?

He was older than Lucy, but always getting into scrapes. Before our grandmother passed away, she made us promise to try and help him. To watch over him. Since I'd been the one taking care of grandma until the end, Lucy told me she'd be the one to keep an eye on him and hopefully help him turn his life around.

She'd stayed close, being a shoulder for him, always willing to give advice or help him out of a jam. It may not have been the healthiest thing, but family was all we had. We had so little of it after our parents died, it seemed like the right thing to do.

I reached past my sister and pulled the door closed behind her, then guided her into my home. I planted a kiss on her head, and gave her one last squeeze, before looking into her big, grey eyes, now bright with tears.

"Let's get you warmed up."

I led her down the hallway, allowing myself a grin as she looked at the opulence all around us—Mr. Drake's family portraits, tapestries and artwork still took my breath away. When we made it to the kitchen, I plunked her down at the large, wooden table, and asked Katja to please make some tea for the two of us.

In a few minutes, I had Lucy's wet coat off, a fire roaring in the kitchen fireplace, and a mug of steaming earl grey in her hands. When she took a deep, shivering sigh, I finally spoke.

"Is it bad news?"

She nodded and took a sip of her tea.

"Are you in trouble?"

I put my hand over hers, urging her to open up. To tell me why she was here on my doorstep, tears running down her pale cheeks.

"It's Alex," she said. "H-he's in deep this time. I don't know how to fix it."

I sighed and put my head in my hands. Of course it was Alex. Wasn't it always?

I pictured the look he'd given me at the wedding, the hungry look in his eyes when he eyed my ring—eyed the man I was about to marry. The look of someone who never had anything, just like me, and vowed to take it from the world, one way or the other.

"Tell me what happened."

"He's locked up, Isa. This time he went too far."

Lucy brushed her wavy hair away from her face, and I longed to reach out and cup her face the way grandma used to do and tell her that it was all going to be okay. But I didn't know that, did I? Not for sure.

"He got caught stealing cars, him and this dumb kid he was hanging around with. I had no idea it was happening until I got the phone call from the police telling me they had him. I just thought he was shooting pool at the bar when he went out at night."

Lucy's eyes plead with her.

"It's not your fault, Luc," I said. "It's not your fault, honey."

I held her hand tighter, and she squeezed back, finally nodding her head.

"But that's not the worst part… Apparently the man he was stealing the cars for… he thinks Alex owes him the price of that job he botched. He was stealing a *Ferrari*, Isa! And now the boss, some guy named Dmitry, wants money each month to make up for what he lost."

Her voice cracked and she stopped, shaking her head. She had another sip of tea.

"Each month?"

"For protection in prison, he says. If I don't pay on Alex's behalf, something bad will happen to him. He's not safe… even where he is."

It was my turn to shake my head. This was one hell of a screwed up situation.

"How much?"

I reached for the purse on the counter, opened it and took out my checkbook. As a partner in Drake Enterprises, I earned a very generous salary. My husband would never know if I passed some of it to my sister.

Lucy's trembling hand on mine stopped me.

"No, Isa. I'm not here for that. You've done too much for us already. Always have."

"Lucy…"

"I couldn't!" Her eyes sparkled again with unshed tears. "I just wanted to know if you have a job available. Something I can do here in the city. The economy dried up most of the good-paying jobs out where we are, and I thought if I could get something better… then maybe everything would be alright."

She hung her head, and I could feel her shame radiating off of her. "I just can't do it on the money I make at the bar. No matter how hard I try."

I bit my lip.

"Of course. I'll talk to Chase and see what we can do."

She leapt up from the table and gave me a hug so tight I thought she might choke me.

"Thank you," she whispered against my neck, her voice fierce with emotion. "Thank you, Isa."

I didn't tell her that I'd also be looking into this Dmitry character with Mr. Drake later on. How could I not? My family was in trouble. There was no way I wasn't going to try to get to the bottom of this, even if it meant paying that bastard off behind her back.

"Can you stay with us tonight? We have plenty of extra rooms and dinner's on soon."

Lucy gave a nervous look around the enormous kitchen and laughed her musical laugh.

"I suppose you would have room, and it is getting dark. I'd love to stay if it's alright," she said shyly. "Just for tonight. I don't want to be too much trouble."

"You're no trouble at all," I said, smiling. "I'll talk to Chase after dinner. We'll get this sorted out."

She nodded and hugged me again. In that moment, I felt the weight of those years of taking care of them on my shoulders again, the burden familiar, but now lighter than it ever was. We could do this, Mr. Drake and I. We could take care of her and Alex.

I'd never thought this before, but now I knew it was good to have resources. It was good to be taken care of and be able to care for those I loved. It was a blessing.

"Come on," I said. "Let's get you something to wear for dinner."

She raised an eyebrow, and it was my turn to laugh as I dragged her up the front staircase to my room.

I'd sent Mr. Daniels to let my husband know about our extra guest and to inform the kitchen. Now, when the doorbell rang, I smiled at my sister, looking radiant with shining red curls and a borrowed cream-colored silk dress. She'd looked at me like I was insane when I said I dressed for dinner now, but that was just the way things were when you lived with a man like Chase Drake.

You better believe all of this opulence took some getting used to, but once I had, I felt more at home because of him, no matter how strange the surroundings. I just thanked my lucky stars each day that I had met such an incredible man, and worked hard to make sure my half of our partnership was well earned.

If there was one thing I learned from my grandma, it was to be useful. To carry your own weight, no matter how blessed you were. I took nothing for granted, and now, seeing it again through Lucy's eyes, made me smile, feeling that happiness again like it was my first day in the home.

I took her hand in mine and we descended the main staircase, me in shimmering blue with my diamond collar, her radiant with opals flashing at her pale throat. When I saw Mr. Drake at the bottom of the stairs in his black suit and tie, my heart did a little flip. Just like my surroundings, I never got used to the fact that he was mine, and that I was his. My gorgeous, dominant Mr. Drake.

Standing next to him was a mysterious man, as dark as Mr. Drake was light. His hair was black, slicked back in a way that made Lucy sigh beside me. I glanced over, my lips quirking into a smile. The stranger's eyes were a piercing blue, his body well built beneath his perfectly cut suit, platinum cufflinks glittering on his cuffs.

"You must be Mr. Pierce. I've heard such good things about you," I said as we reached the bottom, and extended my hand to him.

"It's a pleasure to meet you, Mrs. Drake."

He shook it firmly, and I grinned, then glanced over at my sister. The stranger's eyes had flitted straight from mine to hers, locking in on her, looking her up and down in a way that I remembered only too well.

"And who is this beautiful creature beside you?"

* * *

I felt out of place in Isabeau's dress, felt like a little girl playing dress up, even though I was only a year younger than the dress' owner. I was completely out of my element here—a girl who left grandma's little tract house and drove to the city in her shitty Datsun, not a girl who ate on actual china and used honest-to-God silverware made with real silver.

This was going to be a strange night.

Although I'd felt a sense of relief at Isa's promise so strong I wanted to weep, I still felt odd inside, like I was intruding into her space, into her new life. I didn't belong here with people like this.

I was just Lucy Willcox, the shy little redhead who read too many books and tried to keep out of trouble in my small town life. Lucy Willcox, who loved her brother, and was trying to fill her big sis's shoes in looking out for him. So many people had left me in life, left me fending for myself, that I felt that role was me trying to protect him from that feeling.

Isabeau looked after me until I was old enough to look after myself and my brother, then she took care of Grandma. Isa was always the strong one, the one destined for more. She was my rock up until a couple of years ago when she moved to the city to get work.

And then it was just me and Alex, living our small town lives with our small town problems. That is, until Alex decided to screw it all up again. And of course I was the one who had to be responsible. Who had to pay the price. Someone had to take care of things, and it looked like that would always be me.

I shouldn't think things like that. Everything will be alright, Lucy. You'll see.

I just prayed something would turn up before it was too late. For both of us.

I felt a little silly walking down the grand staircase side by side with Isabeau, like someone playing princess. She'd done my hair up in curls, and I had to admit, I'd liked the way the silk of her dress hung on my slim curves. I didn't often dress up. Where would I go if I did? One of the two bars in town? Maybe the bowling alley or the Laundr-o-mat?

I allowed myself a secret smile at the thought of entering Murphy's, the bar I waited tables in, decked out like this. The usual drunks would stare, and Buck Murphy's toothless old mouth would drop wide open. They'd never believe it was me.

I'd walk right up to him and tell him I wasn't working Sundays any more, a girl had the right to a day off every now and then, and he'd sputter, wondering how to say no to such a regal young woman. Everyone knows you have to do what princesses say or it's "off with your head!" At least that would be how the world worked. It was my fantasy, after all.

My thoughts were interrupted by the sight of Isabeau's new husband, Chase Drake looking truly regal at the bottom of the stairs in a smart suit, but my mouth dropped open when I saw the man standing beside him. He had wavy, dark hair that stuck out just below his ears like a rock star, or maybe an underwear model, with eyes so blue I shivered just looking at them. He looked like a wolf in men's clothing, standing there with one hand tucked into his suit jacket, the cut of his clothing hugging a body that was obviously muscular, tall, and drool-worthy.

And he was looking right at me, the smile on his face hungry, like the wolf looking at little red riding hood. If I got too close, would he gobble me up?

I heard Isabeau say something next to me, and watched as she shook his hand. Then, his intense gaze was focused back on me, trailing down my body in a way that made me want to cover up, even though I was fully dressed, but also made me want to strip down right then and there if that's what he wanted.

Did I just think that?

His eyes met mine, a blue like the depths of a glacier—cold and hard as ice.

"And who is this beautiful creature beside you?"

He didn't look back at my sister as she answered him, introducing me, I suppose. Everything was a blur then except for his beautiful face; his gaze meeting mine. His cheekbones looked like they were carved from marble, his jaw strong and proud, the planes of his shoulders broad and powerful. He exuded confidence in a way I'd never seen before, except maybe from Mr. Drake.

This was not a man to be trifled with. That much was clear. And something glinting deep in those shocking eyes said he was also a man who knew exactly what he wanted, and got it every time.

I heard my name dimly and held out my hand, my pale skin trembling as I reached toward this stranger, this mysterious man, standing a head taller than I was, dominating the space like he owned the whole place.

"It's a pleasure," he said, his voice low and deep, the words caressing me like an intimate touch.

When our skin met, it was electric. I tried not to tremble as he drew my hand up to his full lips, lips I wanted to run my tongue over, lips I wanted on my mouth, my neck, my *everywhere*. He planted a hot kiss on my skin, and I heard a small sound escape my mouth like a whimper.

Embarrassment rushed through me as I realized I was staring like a complete dolt. Like an idiot schoolgirl with a crush. Like a child playing princess who just met a real, honest-to-God prince and stared until her eyes bugged out and her mother had to shoo her away.

I felt the heat coloring my cheeks and I looked away, ashamed.

"Pleasure to meet you as well," I said, bobbing my head.

Oh, my God. Why didn't I just flipping curtsy while I was at it?

I wanted to die. This was worse than meeting the captain of the football team when you were just a silly little chess nerd, a fantasy paperback tucked under your arm. At that moment, I wished the immaculate floor would just give way and swallow me right on up.

It would have been a mercy.

"If you please," Mr. Daniels said, from the edge of the foyer. "Dinner is served in the dining room."

He gestured with a white-gloved hand and Isabeau tugged me along. The men followed, but not before I saw the bemused expression on Maxwell Pierce's handsome face. He thought I was a joke. I put my hand to my cheek, wondering how I was going to sit through a whole dinner without making a fool of myself.

I never was very good at hiding my emotions. Sometimes I felt I blushed at the drop of a hat.

Ugh.

We entered the dining room, and I gasped at the finery all around me. Crisp, white linens and a gleaming silver service shone between tapered candles in polished candlesticks. A giant oil painting nearly covered one wall, modern slashes of color and darkness making the room seem less old-fashioned than it could, and hopelessly luxurious.

I sat in the chair Isa offered, and swallowed hard as Mr. Pierce took the seat just opposite. He gave me a lopsided smile as he tucked his napkins onto his lap, then leaned back, tenting his fingers on his knees as he looked me over. His gaze was cool. Assessing. Like he was deciding what I was made of. Was I a good girl or a very, very bad one?

Watching him watching me, I suddenly didn't know the answer myself. His slender fingers beneath his chin looked like they were made for trailing over a woman's curves. Made for brushing hair aside, for unbuttoning blouses and letting them fall to the floor.

I felt myself blushing again, and swore inwardly.

"So," said Chase Drake, creating the diversion I'd been silently willing to happen. "What brings you visiting, Max? Work, or did you just miss me?"

He grinned at his friend and clapped him on the shoulder.

"A little of both, actually," he said, looking straight at me. "I'm sure you, of all people, can understand mixing business with pleasure."

"Ah, yes. I see now," Chase said. "You're here because you've already burned through every woman at the company?"

Mr. Daniels filled my wine glass, and I looked at him gratefully before taking a long swallow. It was very good. White. That was about as far as I knew my wines, but at this time all I wanted was a buzz.

What does he mean, burned through every woman?

"Hardly," Mr. Pierce said, with a cool smile. "Just all of the ones I wanted."

His lips quirked into a grin, and Chase laughed, shaking his head.

"Same old Maxwell."

Isabeau cleared her throat. I looked over and saw her blush as well. The little knot that had formed in my stomach loosened just a little. She looked desperate to change the subject.

"On a different note… I was just wondering. Do you know of any open positions at Drake Enterprises? Lucy's looking for work right now, and I wanted to see what we might be able to find for her."

Mr. Drake looked at his wife with kind eyes, then over at me. I wanted to shrink down into my seat to avoid that searching gaze.

"Well, what kind of work are you interested in, Lucy? I'm sure we'll be able to find something that would be a good fit."

"Um…" Suddenly, my mouth seemed drier than a cow skull baking in the desert heat. "I have some experience with office work… Administration and… and such."

I didn't exactly bend the truth. I'd done the books often enough for Buck when he was too drunk to make the numbers add up at the end of the month. 'Invaluable,' he'd called me. That counted. Right?

Maxwell Pierce leaned forward, his eyes locked on me like a snake about to strike.

"As it happens, I have a position open," he said, his voice sliding over me like an oil slick.

I sipped my wine again and tried not to shiver beneath that look.

"I came here to ask Chase for a recommendation. Someone he might know who could perform the particular duties I require." He glanced over at his friend, and an odd sort of look passed between them. "As it so happens, I'm in need of a personal assistant."

Isabeau choked beside me, covering her mouth as she coughed on a mouthful of wine.

"The salary is far above the market average, but I have special requirements my assistants must meet in exchange."

At that moment, Mr. Daniels came through the doors with the first course, a beautiful plate of what looked like pate. I'd never had pate before, but I'd always been curious.

"Let's not discuss business over dinner," Isabeau said.

I looked at her, wondering why she'd stopped the discussion. Maybe Mr. Pierce's offer was the answer to my prayers. Maybe it was just what I, and Alex needed, and she wouldn't have to save the day, yet again. Maybe I could take care of myself without needing Big Sister's help, just this once. And wouldn't that be exactly perfect?

The men agreed and dug in, but once in a while during the conversation, I could feel Maxwell Pierce's eyes on me—always watching. Assessing. Studying me like I was a puzzle that needed solving.

And what was even stranger, was that I liked it.

I sipped my wine and ate, wondering what kind of man he was, and wondering what kind of woman he saw in me.

"She's too young!"

I heard Isabeau's rough whisper from behind the door of the wood-paneled library, and stopped briefly to listen on my way back from freshening up in the bathroom.

"You said she's only a year younger than you are, my dear."

"But she doesn't know what he means! She doesn't understand all that's… well, *involved.*"

"Did you?"

There was an odd, weighty silence, and I tip-toed past, not wanting to get in the middle of their arguing.

In the lounge adjoining the dining room, I found Maxwell Pierce in a wingback chair, sipping brandy by the fire. He looked up as I entered, and smiled that eerie smile of his, his handsome face at once almost too gorgeous to look at and not a little frightening.

"Lucy. Please," he said, gesturing to the chair across from him. "Join me, won't you?"

The way he said it, I wasn't sure if it was a request or a command. I sat down, and accepted the brandy he poured for me gratefully.

"I was serious, you know. About needing an assistant. I think you'd be perfect for the job."

I swallowed hard. "But how do you know?"

He tilted his head, gazing at me like an innocent who didn't quite understand a joke that had just been told.

"I'm very good at knowing," was all the answer he gave. "I'd need you to start right away. I fly back home tomorrow."

I nodded, thinking of the meager two suitcases that currently held all my worldly belongings, sitting in my room upstairs. I'd had them in the car, ready to go apartment hunting here after staying the night in a hotel, but since Isa offered her home, here I was.

"May I ask… I mean to say," I began.

I was always terrible at this part. How do you ask someone like this about money? Did they have any idea how important it was to someone like me? Or would I look as crass as I felt just thinking about it?

"You want to know what the pay is, of course."

Mr. Pierce took a small pad of paper and a pen from an inner pocket of his jacket, and wrote a number on it before folding it and handing it over to me. I opened it and my hand flew to my mouth.

"This *much*? Per year?"

I could hardly believe my luck. This was twice as much as I made at the bar. It was absolutely perfect. Absolutely what Alex and I needed to get out of his mess.

"Per month."

I tried to speak, but all that came out was a funny little "whoosh" of breath. Mr. Pierce chuckled and sat back in his chair.

"Is that a yes?"

I swallowed hard and took a sip of the brandy. The liquor was sweet but burned at the same time, just like the idea of making all of that money. What strings were attached to such an offer?

"W-what would my responsibilities be? Exactly?"

He cocked his head at me as if looking at a new species beneath a microscope.

"Smart girl," he said. "There is a contract I'll need you to sign before you begin working for me. I am a man of particular tastes, and my personal assistant needs to cater to those tastes. Those... needs. It's not your every day job, to be sure." His eyes burned into mine, reflecting the firelight. "But I think you'll enjoy it."

I sat back, wondering what kind of tastes this powerful man meant, and if I could provide for them. A little chill went through me as I wondered if maybe this was some kind of sexual thing. Would I be selling myself to this man? Was that why the pay was so high?

As if reading my mind, he spoke again.

"My assistants always live with me, so you would be at my beck and call night and day, seven days a week."

His beck and call...

"I would require you to wear a uniform of my choosing, and it may change from day to day, depending on my mood. You would only wear what I gave you to wear. You wouldn't bring any of your own clothing along. I would provide for your every need."

I nodded as if all of this made sense. As if it were all perfectly normal. But I suspected my face betrayed my confusion.

He'd control what I wore? Even... even my underwear?

"And of course you would see things on the job—confidential things—which would require your discretion."

"I can do that," I said, looking down at the impossible string of numbers on the paper again.

Maxwell Pierce took a sip of his brandy, and I couldn't help but admire that sensual mouth of his once again. He licked his lips and smiled, and I turned away, as if caught in some sinful act.

"I can get the contract from my room, if you'd like to look it over tonight. I'm leaving tomorrow, like I said, so I'd need your answer soon."

"That... that would be great, Mr. Pierce."

"Good girl, Lucy," he said.

He stood and handed me his brandy before sweeping out of the room. I took it without question, holding it for him like I was already on the job. I sat, staring into the fire, wondering what on earth I was getting myself into, and if I was rushing things. Unbidden, I saw the plexiglass over the visitors desk, my brother's pale face behind it, holding the phone to his ear as he begged me for help.

"God, I'm so sorry, Luc," he said, his voice cracking. "But if we don't pay, I don't know what's going to happen to me in here. I… I just don't know what they'd do to me. Please, sis. *Please.* I need you."

I sipped from my glass and forced myself to hold back the tears stinging my eyes. I had to do this, no matter what this man's bizarre expectations were. I had to do it for him. And this way was so much better than imposing on Isa, who'd already given this family so much. It was my turn to step up. My turn to be strong.

I vowed to do it, if I had the courage. I had to. For them.

Mr. Pierce appeared from the shadows, and I jumped, startled. He took his drink back and dropped a thick stack of paper in my lap. The contract.

"Read it over, Lucy. And if you like what you read, come to see me right away. Even if it's the middle of the night, you won't disturb me. I'm interested in hearing your answer as soon as possible."

I nodded and rose from my chair. "Thank you. I'll go look it over right now."

Mr. Pierce's hand shot out and grabbed my wrist. His hold was gentle, but firm.

"Any time tonight, Lucy. I mean it."

He brushed his thumb over my wrist, and I felt a heat stirring low in my belly at the touch. This man was so strange, so demanding, but so intoxicating at the same time. When I looked at him, I felt the same giddy feeling in the pit of my stomach as a person does looking over a ledge and wondering what it would be like to jump.

In that moment, I knew he was dangerous, but I didn't think I could help myself. I vowed to sign the contract, no matter what it said. And I'd do it tonight, before Isabeau could stop me.

After a quick word to Isa and a kiss on the cheek, I'd made my excuses and gone to bed, and by "gone to bed," I of course mean "snuck upstairs to read the contract."

I now paused in my reading, my mouth dropping open in a little 'o' of surprise. I'd passed the peculiar verbiage on dressing the way Mr. Pierce decided, and had gotten to a startling passage titled "Punishment."

PUNISHMENT

The assistant agrees to the employer punishing her whenever he sees fit in whatever manner he sees fit, along the following guidelines:

Punishments can hurt, but will not harm the assistant or leave any permanent mark on her person. Punishments will be given while assistant is clothed unless the assistant consents to an unclothed punishment, and may at any time use her *safety word to halt the punishment.

*SAFETY

The assistant shall choose a safety word to use whenever she sees fit in order to stop any and all punishments given by the employer. The safety word shall be communicated to the employer and not changed by the assistant without the employer's knowledge in order to secure her safety and comfort. No punishments shall be administered without both parties knowing the assistant's safety word.

TERMINATING THIS CONTRACT

This is an At Will position which can be terminated by the employer or assistant at any time. The termination notification must be given in writing, but can be done without prior notice or advance warning. If the contract is terminated by the employer, and the assistant has not breached the terms of this contract, the employer will pay a severance fee of an additional two months' salary and reimburse the assistant for all travel expenses. If the assistant terminates the contract, she will be reimbursed for all travel expenses and paid for the last full week of work.

I sat back on the four-poster bed, nestled in the silk pillows, wide-eyed and feeling dazed.

This was most *definitely* some kind of weird sex thing, even if I was with my clothes on. Clothes picked by him, as well! This was some seriously kinky shit. Punishments? Safety words? What the hell?

I'd read about this kind of thing before in romance novels, but I'd certainly never experienced it. The punishments would hurt, but not harm? What could that mean?

Images of Mr. Pierce bending me over his knee and hitting me with the palm of his hand flew through my mind. Would he caress me first, or just spank me hard until tears rolled down my face and I was gasping for breath? And what's more, would I like it?

I rolled over onto my knees and gave myself an exploratory swat on the butt. Tears pricked my eyes, but this time it was from a case of the giggles I suddenly didn't feel like I could contain. This was *too much.* It was too weird, and I was too desperate to pass it up. I couldn't pass it up.

I sat back down and gazed at the contract. Suddenly, the giggles subsided, and all I could think about was Mr. Pierce's face as he looked at me, really looked at me, those haunting eyes of his sliding down over my body in Isabeau's dress; approval and hunger glinting in their depths. And suddenly, it struck me.

He wanted me.

The ache between my thighs as I thought of him made me realize I wanted him too. I'd wanted him since I'd first seen him at the bottom of that staircase. But girls like me didn't get to want men like him. He was from a whole other world, an upper echelon of heroes and angels and devils far above us mere mortals.

He was too beautiful, too rich, too… everything.

But he was also offering me something I couldn't, something I wouldn't, refuse. A way to help Alex. A way to get us back on our feet without bothering the sister I owed so much to. A way to become the woman I wanted to be. A provider. A giver. Not just another mouth to feed.

I needed to accept, no matter what the cost.

I flipped to the last page of the contract and signed my name, feeling as I did so, like I was signing in blood. A part of me knew that something like this was bound to change my life forever, but right now, I didn't care. Something had to change, and the sooner, the better. For everyone.

I paused, my hand raised, ready to knock on Mr. Pierce's door when I heard a peculiar noise coming from inside. There was a groan, and the sound of flesh on flesh, then a noise like a grunt. I edged closer, pressing my ear to the door. I knew I shouldn't be eavesdropping, but what was going on? Was Mr. Pierce hurt?

Then, I heard a single word that made me blush from the roots of my hair straight down to my toes, bare on the thick hallway carpet.

"Lucy…"

I heard a slapping noise, the pace becoming more rhythmic, more frantic as I listened, and suddenly, I understood what I was hearing.

Maxwell Pierce was touching himself, just beyond that door. Touching himself—running his hands over his hard body… gripping himself in his strong fist… getting himself off while thinking of *me*.

I stood still, hardly daring to breathe, my hands pressed against the door, as if by getting closer, I could almost see what was going on in Mr. Pierce's private moment. I imagined what he might look like, standing naked and proud in front of the mirror, or maybe lying back on the bed, his shaft standing erect and huge as he slid his hand over it, the other cupping his balls, imagining that it was my hand, or my mouth or…

The door opened so fast, I almost fell, and I shrieked as I gripped the doorframe for balance. Mr. Pierce stood in the doorway, his face unreadable, holding nothing but a cotton robe in one fist, the drape of the fabric barely covering his nudity.

I gaped at him, unable to even apologize, as my eyes traveled down his body. His arms and chest were muscular, his shoulders wide and strong, but it was the bead of sweat rolling gently down his chiseled abs toward the place where he held the robe that really caught my interest. I could see a dusting of dark hair over his pecs, leading to a devastatingly sexy trail, going down, down, down…

"Miss Willcox," he snapped.

I met his eyes, shame coiling inside of me. What was worse, eavesdropping on such a private moment, or ogling this poor man like he was the centerfold of Playgirl?

Drop the towel, I thought, and then bit my lip, hardly daring to meet his gaze, but unable to stop myself.

"I… I signed the contract," I stammered, my voice high and small.

His mouth didn't move, but I thought I saw a smile in those mesmerizing eyes.

"Come in."

He turned, swinging the robe over his shoulders, but not before I got a spectacular view of his muscular backside.

Keep cool, Lucy, and for God's sake, stop staring!

He belted the robe on tight and I turned away, shutting the door behind me.

He sat on the bed, and nodded toward a chair by the vanity. I sat and handed him the contract. He looked it over, nodding as he saw my dated signature, then grinning up at me.

"So, we have a deal, I see?"

"Mm hmm," I said, suddenly feeling very sweaty and very, very out of place.

"No questions about any part of the contract before you begin working for me?"

Questions? Nawww, what would I have questions about? The punishments? Or maybe the fact that you will be choosing my clothing all the way down to which thong I put on under my skirt? Or what about the fact that you seem more like a weird, kinky perv than a boss??

"Nope," I squeaked.

He stared at me for a long while; long enough that I squirmed in the chair, wishing I'd worn more than my thin cotton nightdress to come see him. Although it wasn't as if I was exactly overdressed, based on how he'd opened the door.

"Excellent," he said. "I trust you can begin immediately?"

"Yes, Sir."

"Good. Very good." He put his finger to his lips, looking me over. "Then tell me which safety word you've chosen."

I paused for a moment, racking my brain. *The safety word…*

"Dmitry," I said, and felt a chill go down my spine.

When I wanted all this to stop, I would say 'Dmitry,' and remind myself why I was doing this in the first place. Why a good girl from a small town would even touch such a contract. Why I would take such a strange job with an even stranger man.

"Dmitry it is," he said, looking at me again in that way that told me I was as much a puzzle to him as he was to me.

"Now, Lucy. I want you to come over here and receive your first punishment."

"What??"

I jumped up from the chair, then sank back down slowly as I saw the look in his eyes.

"You were spying on me, little Lucy. I know you were listening to me behind that door. That was very, very naughty of you. I think you know that."

I opened my mouth to protest, but knew I'd been caught. Caught like a rat in a trap. After all… I did sign the contract, and I did just say I could begin immediately. And I had been spying.

The thought made me writhe inside with embarrassment. This was not the little girl my family raised! I didn't do things like spying on gorgeous men, and I certainly would never have lied about it if I did. I had to face what was coming.

"Yes, Sir," I whispered.

"I like that, Lucy. I like that you call me 'Sir.' Let's keep it that way."

I nodded, looking down at my hands in my lap.

"Now. Come here to me."

I stood and moved hesitantly, stepping slowly toward him until I stood before the bed, eye-to-eye with this sexy, frightening man.

He reached out and gently brushed my hair back over my shoulders, his gaze softening as he looked me over. I could practically feel the heat radiating off him, and could see his naked chest through the gap in his robe. Knowing he was nude under there, so close I could just reach down and touch him, made a throbbing begin between my legs. I'd never had a lot of experience with men, and most certainly nothing like this.

To say Mr. Pierce was different than my bumpkin of a high school sweetheart was the understatement of the year.

"You've been very bad, Lucy, violating my privacy like that. Do you understand?"

I nodded, feeling low down and dirty, but at the same time wondering why he'd told me to come by in the night if he was going to be doing… well… *that.*

He pulled me close, his strong hands gripping my waist. I could feel his breath tickling my neck, and turned my head to the side, suddenly very afraid.

What would he do to me? Would he take me here and now? Would he do that without my go ahead? Just what had I agreed to when I said I'd be at his beck and call?

"This is the beginning of your training, little Lucy," he whispered in my ear. "If you're going to work for me, you must follow my rules."

"But…"

"You'll get to know me, my dear, and you'll learn my likes and dislikes. You'll learn to anticipate what I want, and what I don't want."

He leaned in closer, so close that our bodies were almost pressed together.

"And you'll learn to love it, even when I have to punish you. Maybe even especially then."

I shrieked as he pulled me down, yanking me over his knees like a child until my hair dangled on the floor and my ass stuck straight up in the air. He held me firm as I squirmed against him, and suddenly, I could feel his erection pressing into my belly.

I gasped, but I didn't push away, didn't fight him, didn't move as I lay across his lap, waiting to see what he would do next.

When he hand came down on my ass with a loud *crack*, I whimpered against him. The sting was sudden and strong—and absolutely nothing like I'd imagined. His hand came down again on the other cheek, and I let out a cry, my body aching even as an undeniable heat built inside of me.

He's spanking me. He's really doing it. Oh, my God, I'm letting him do it!

His hand came down again and again, on first one cheek, then the other, lightly at first, then harder, until I moaned, the sharp pain transforming with each touch of his hand on my bottom, slowly becoming something else. Something altogether alien and altogether sexual. I realized I was wet, my thighs glistening below my thin nightgown. I wondered if he could tell… If he knew what this was doing to me. If he could smell me, or feel a wet spot growing on my nightgown.

He smacked me again harder and harder, drawing moans and wails from me, the pain pleasure, the pleasure pain almost unendurable, each loud slap making my core pulse. I felt his erection twitch beneath me, and wondered what it was like for him, seeing me bent over, knowing my ass was reddening with each strike; knowing that my skin would be tender, bruised even, in such an intimate place.

Then, just as quickly as it began, it was over, and his hands were kneading my flesh, making me moan in a new way, his strong hands massaging away the hurt, soothing my inflamed skin, his touch as gentle now as it had been harsh.

"You're going to remember this little lesson each time you sit tomorrow, little Lucy," he said. His voice was a low growl. "You're going to think of me during the flight, as you shift from side to side. And you're going to remember this night."

I trembled against his legs and realized tears I didn't know I'd shed were wetting my cheeks. He pulled me up so I stood shaking in front of him, then pulled me onto his lap. He held me to his chest then, stroking my hair as my breathing evened and my tears dried. I could smell the spicy scent of his aftershave, and flushed as I felt his cheek against mine.

After a little while he stood and set me on my feet again.

"Goodnight, Lucy. Nothing more tonight."

I stared at him, numb with the shock of the evening, until I finally came to my senses and turned toward the door. I paused before I touched the knob and looked back, but he was gone. I heard the sink running in the bathroom, and knew I had been dismissed. He was truly done with me for the night, just like that.

Later, as I lay in bed, biting my lip as my fingers stroked my aching clit, my core on fire as my tender ass rubbed against the sheets, I thought of that glimpse I'd gotten before the robe hid him from view. My boss' tight, muscular body was against mine in my fantasies, his hands on me instead of my own, that stiff, hot rod that I'd felt beneath my belly was inside of me, stroking in and out, driving me wild as he took me again and again.

As he fucked me and made me *his*.

I cried out as I came, and wondered if he knew. If he knew how crazy he'd made me, even though I'd been so afraid. Even though I hadn't wanted it to be that way. At least… not at first.

I lay in bed a long while, staring at the ceiling, wondering if this really was a business relationship or the beginning of something so much more. The thought was at once terrifying and alluring. Little Lucy was finally doing something wild. Something dangerous.

And, just maybe, something that could save my brother's life.

I finally fell asleep on my stomach, and dreamed of Mr. Pierce's cool blue gaze watching me.

Chapter Two

Isabeau

"How could she just leave, without a word? Without waiting for me to help her?"

I sipped my coffee with shaking hands, the ball of worry in my throat so big I could barely breath. Mr. Drake reached across the kitchen table and grabbed my hand, holding me, letting me know he was there.

"According to Mr. Daniels, she and Maxwell left early this morning, suitcases in hand." He frowned down at his own coffee. "I should have seen this coming. Maxwell is used to getting what he wants. He moves fast."

"But why couldn't she just let us help? Why did she go to him instead of her own sister?"

Mr. Drake stood and pulled me up out of my chair, before holding me in his strong arms. His robe was soft against my cheek, his body hard as he held me tight.

"Maybe she wanted to do this herself, Isa. Maybe that was exactly why she didn't wait for your help."

I looked up at him, my beautiful Mr. Drake, and saw understanding in his eyes. I thought of all the times I'd taken care of Lucy and Alex after our parents passed away. I was basically the head of the household, even though I was only a year older than my sister. I'd taken the brunt of the responsibility… but had that left her feeling like a child all these years?

"Will he hurt her?"

That was my greatest fear. That even though Maxwell Pierce was a friend of my husband's, he might be too much of a billionaire playboy—careless with women in the extreme. That he might break my dear sister's heart in a way she wasn't prepared for.

And worst of all, that he wouldn't be able to help her save Alex. Not like I could. Not like Mr. Drake could. We had to get involved, no matter what Lucy wanted. There was simply no other option.

"He…" Mr. Drake trailed off. "I hope not. Let me just say that. Maxwell may be promiscuous, but he's a good man, deep down."

He kissed my hair and I sighed against him, leaning on him for strength.

"I just hope he hasn't changed too much in these years we were apart. I hope he's still the man I befriended."

Mr. Drake sat back down and pulled me gently into his lap, holding me tight, and in that moment, I knew I had to tell him everything. I needed him if I was going to find out about this Dmitry character. I needed him to know the dark parts of my past—about Alex and his troubled youth. I needed to know if he could help me, even if it meant paying off a criminal.

Guilt bubbled up inside of me, and I let out a sob. I couldn't help myself. It was all too much, too fast. Not only was I worried sick about my sister, but my brother's life was at stake. And now I was putting Mr. Drake in the middle of it.

"Tell me, Isa," he said. "Tell me everything."

I nodded, one of my tears falling down onto my husband's cheek, and did as I was told.

Lucy

Well, he'd been right about the flight.

While Mr. Pierce had taken a pill with his scotch and pulled a sleep mask down over his eyes, I'd shifted from side to side, my bruised, tender bottom making me bite my lip each time I felt a twinge of pain. It was only a three-hour flight, but each jolt, each stab each time I rubbed the wrong way, made it seem like an eternity. Thank God he'd sprung for first class seats. I couldn't imagine being cooped up in coach with a bottom as red as a baboon's chafing on the cheap upholstery.

I sipped a glass of wine and wondered what my new life would be like, as Mr. Pierce's personal assistant. Would it be glamorous and exciting? Or had I just made a terrible mistake trusting this man? I knew I had brains, but what if I wasn't qualified? What if doing the books for old Buck Murphy was child's play compared to assisting a businessman of his caliber?

I chewed my lip, hoping I was cut out for the job. I knew I wasn't much to look at now, and suddenly, was very, very glad that controlling my wardrobe had been part of Maxwell Pierce's stipulations. Thinking of showing up at the office, representing such a magnetic, powerful man, wearing my best jean skirt and floral blouse made my cheeks heat. It was good enough for home, but would never be good enough in an office like his. Hopefully he would save me from such humiliation, for both our sakes.

At baggage claim, Mr. Pierce stood, making phone calls in a bored-sounding voice as I fetched his expensive luggage and the two shabby bags I'd brought along, not that I'd be able to use much in them. Hopefully I'd be able to at least bust out my favorite cowgirl boots on the weekends.

Except I'll be at his beck and call 24/7. Right…

I'd momentarily forgotten that this contract didn't exactly include weekends. Then again, what did it include? All it really specified were punishments and wardrobe control. Everything else was a bit of a grey area.

I strained to get the bag off the carousel, huffing and puffing as I dragged it up over the edge and dropped it to the ground. When I looked over, I saw Mr. Pierce staring at me with this odd little smile, as if he hadn't really expected me to do what he'd asked and was pleasantly surprised that I did.

I tossed my hair and brushed off my jeans. Did he think I wasn't capable? Just because I was petite, didn't mean I hadn't done my share of hard, manual labor throughout my lifetime.

Did he think I was weak or something? Or had his previous assistants just turned up their noses when faced with such tasks?

I held my head high as I stacked one bag on top of the rolling suitcase and tied it on, then hefted the other beneath my arm. I'd show him a thing or two. If he was paying this much for me, then by God, he was going to get one hell of a hard worker. That's how our grandparents raised us, and that's how I was going to live, weird-ass contract or not.

"Are you ready, Sir?"

He nodded, bemused, and I let him lead the way in his immaculate suit, allowing myself a good, long look at his incredibly sexy backside as I dragged the bags along, bumping over the airport carpet.

One thing was for sure. This job was going to be interesting.

"There must be some kind of mix-up, Ma'am," I said to the portly blonde woman who'd led me up to my room. "This place is bigger than my gran's entire house… Mr. Pierce wanted you to take me to *my* room."

The housekeeper gave me a look that said *Oh, you poor, innocent little thing*, and turned to leave.

"Hey, wait!"

My bags were already on the enormous four-poster bed, so her job was apparently done. She had deposited me exactly where Mr. Pierce wanted me, and was headed down the hall toward a dark, back stairwell leading God-knows-where.

This house, if you could even call it that, made me feel like I'd been swallowed by a giant. I wasn't exactly expecting my new digs to be in some kind of modern-day-castle, perched on a hill overlooking the city, surrounded by hedges thicker than my car and meticulously maintained.

This was insane. I already felt like I stuck out like a sore thumb. In a place like this, I stood an excellent chance of getting lost on the way to the bathroom and never being seen or heard from again.

I sighed and closed the door. I supposed I'd better get used to this house if I wanted to keep my new job. I needed this position —Alex needed it—so I'd better adjust my attitude and learn how to live in this behemoth of a mansion. Visions of trailing breadcrumbs behind me swum behind my eyes, and I let out a tired laugh.

Something on the bed buzzed to life, and I jumped, but instead of the worlds-biggest-beetle, the noise came from a sleek, black tablet phone, words flashing on the screen.

Meet me in the drawing room immediately to discuss your uniform.

There was no "from," or a signature. But did there need to be? Obviously this was Mr. Pierce's warm way of welcoming to me into his home and making me feel at ease in my new position… Yeah, *right.*

I sighed and moved to the large mirror over the carved, wooden vanity. My hair was a mess of curls after the flight, but there was nothing I could do about that now. He did say "immediately." I blew a flyaway out of my face, finger combed the worst parts, gave up, and left the room, phone in hand.

Looking down the long hallway, modern abstract art lining the walls, I realized I had no freaking clue where the drawing room was. Or even what a drawing room was. Was it an art room? A room for drawing baths? (Heaven forbid.) Or maybe it was one of those big useless rooms full of chaise lounges that wasn't *for* anything…

Jesus Christ, I did not belong here.

I made my way to the end of the hall, passing a doorway that looked like it led to another wing of the house, and peeped into the dark stairwell the housekeeper had gone down. Her round face stared up at me from the bottom of the stairs, and I stifled a giggle as I saw her glare. She was sneaking a cigarette, blowing the smoke out of a tiny side-window on the landing.

"Servants only," she hissed in an Irish accent.

I pressed my lips together and skedaddled back the way I'd come. I was no snitch, and this was definitely not the way I wanted to go.

The phone buzzed in my hand.

What part of "immediately" was unclear, Lucy?

I trotted back down the hallway, little waves of anxiety rippling through me now, searching for the right way to go.

He knows I don't know his floor plan, right? He knows I didn't get the tour, right? He cares about facts like that… right?

Part of me wondered if this was like the first night—a trap to make me break rules he hadn't set quite yet.

What a bastard.

I poked my head through the doorway I'd passed before, and just as I suspected, it led to another hallway, further into the depths of the house. This place was like Downton-Abbey-huge. It was ridiculous for one man to live this way. Didn't he get lost? Lonely? Didn't he get cold in such a big, spooky old castle all by himself?

I had to admit, as I snuck through a variety of halls, peeking into room after room, that it was all impeccably decorated. A beautiful mix of antiques, old portraits, and modern touches like sleek sculpture and slim-line furniture made the place inviting, although still dreadfully intimidating.

I passed what looked like the library from Beauty and the Beast (I'll be back for you, room!), a billiard room (am I in the house from Clue?), what looked like a conservatory (Oh, God, I'm going to get murdered with a candlestick), several rooms that looked like different varieties of studies, dens and storage spaces, when I saw light from up ahead, and realized I'd reached the rooms in the front-facing part of the home. I stood at the entrance to the foyer, and gave a little jump for joy when I saw a cracked door off to the left, and spotted a suited arm peeking out on the rest of a wingback.

Bingo.

I rapped on the doorjamb, and Mr. Pierce swiveled toward me, away from the fireplace. He raised an eyebrow.

"What on earth took you so long, Lucy? Did you stop for a game of pool on the way?"

I blushed, and repressed a scowl.

"No, Sir."

"Then what was it, Lucy? I asked to see you immediately, and immediately is what I meant. Is this any way to make an impression your first full day on the job?"

The look on his face was inscrutable, but the twinkle in those sharp blue eyes of his gave him away. He was loving this.

I wanted to growl in frustration, and if I'd been back at the bar, I would have given old Buck an earful. But, then again, Buck wouldn't be pissing me off like this. He could be a bear once in a while, but he always meant well. Unlike some bosses I could mention.

"I got lost, Sir," I said through gritted teeth.

"Lost, Lucy?" He made a *tisk-tisk* sound and smiled. "Why didn't you use the map of the house I'd left on your phone?"

I felt the heat creeping up my neck, but instead of embarrassment, I was more annoyed than I'd been in years. More annoyed than when Alex would come in at 3 a.m. and bang the door closed behind him. More annoyed than when I served a rowdy table of twelve and got stiffed on the tip. More annoyed than…

"I expect you to be prompt from now on, understood? I am not a man who enjoys being kept waiting."

He grinned then, his fingers tented just beneath his chin, his beautiful black hair falling in a superman curl over his forehead. I wanted to brush it off for him. I wanted to kick him. I wanted to fall into his lap.

Goddamn, this man was frustrating!

"Yes, Sir. No problem, Sir."

No matter how aggravating or deliciously tempting my new boss was, I couldn't get on his bad side. I needed to keep this job no matter what, or Alex was in a world of hurt. I wouldn't be able to live with myself if anything happened to him, especially if it was my fault for bringing it down on him.

The way Mr. Pierce was looking at me made it hard not to fidget. It was that hunter's look again, like I was prey, trembling in his sights, and he could smell the hot blood pumping through my veins. Like he wondered what I would taste like when he finally caught me.

"Good girl," he said. "Now, about the uniform I'd like you to wear in the office tomorrow, and the one I'd like you to wear around this house... You will wear garters and thigh-high stockings at all times, as well as heels at least 3" high, unless I specify otherwise."

My eyes widened, but I smartly kept my trap shut.

He whisked a credit card out of his side pocket, and stared at me pointedly.

"Please find some tasteful heels and garters today. Only buy in the colors red, black, white or pink, both hosiery and shoes, understand?"

I nodded, my mouth so dry I didn't know if I could protest even if I had the will. So he really wanted me to trot around in heels and garters, huh? Yep, this wasn't weirdly sexual at all... But part of me was already imagining the look in his eyes when he caught a glimpse of my bare thigh above the garter, of the way his eyes would travel down my leg. My core heated at the thought, and as sick as I knew it was, a part of me couldn't wait.

"As for the rest of your attire, I have a few things for you to try on. I wasn't sure of your exact size, but I have a variety here, and we can order more as soon as we know what suits you."

I nodded, stunned that he'd already picked things out. Had he called ahead before we even left? He was very resourceful.

He stood and gestured toward an adjoining room, that I realized was a large bathroom, right off the drawing room. There was a rack of clothing in there looking small against the wide, stone tiled floor. I knew nothing should surprise me here, but the fact that one of his "half baths" was bigger than my kitchen was not exactly lost on me.

"Go try on a skirt and blouse first, and come out for approval when you're ready with the best fit."

I nodded, stunned, and did as I was told, moving into the humongous bathroom and shutting the door behind me with a *click*. The first thing I noticed, besides the gorgeous claw-footed bathtub set in front of a wide, curtained window, was that Mr. Pierce had also included bras and panties in the mix hanging on the rack.

As far as I knew, you couldn't return underwear once someone had purchased it… and there were a variety of sizes right in the ballpark of my firm, but modest, breasts and posterior.

How observant, I thought, and how wasteful.

The tags were still on, prices carefully snipped off, so I picked through carefully. Perhaps I could return the rest later, since I was his assistant, and save him some dough. Looking at the luxurious silk, lace and beautiful construction, I might be able to get back thousands of dollars, just for the underwear.

I didn't even want to know how much money he'd spent on this little bathroom changing room, and I tried not to feel ill, thinking of how much bone marrow I'd have to sell to even buy 1/3 of the things in here.

I slipped into a dove-grey bra and panty set and kicked my old underthings into the corner. The fit was perfect, the balconette giving me some serious cleavage. I hadn't worn anything more than a J.C. Penney bra in as long as I could remember, and I was surprised at how good the girls could look with the right help.

I slid on a tight, black pencil skirt, and let out a whimper as I bent to brush it down straight—there was a slit going all the way up the thigh, invisible until I bent over. I shook my head. Of *course* there was. I'd have to be careful at work not to let this naughty little secret show. If anyone was going to get a peek at my hosiery, I definitely didn't want it to be some random lady from accounting or the dude who delivered the break room snacks.

I tried not to let my embarrassment get the best of me, imagining nightmare scenarios of tripping and falling in the hallway, my skirt riding up until my panties showed, the whole office goggling and laughing and pointing and…

Whatever. Shake it off, Lucy. Just try on the damn clothes.

The blouses were beautiful—timeless short-sleeved button ups with silk ties that draped just below a glimpse of cleavage. I felt like a 40's pin up in danger of being nudified if the stiffest breeze kicked up… and I have to admit—I sort of liked it. I'd never considered myself "sexy," had always just been cute, or girl-next-door. This was a new feeling altogether, and, sweeping my hair up experimentally on top of my head, I was enjoying it.

Sexy Lucy, I thought, and repressed a giggle. Who would have bet on it?

I took a deep breath and stepped out of the bathroom. Mr. Pierce was lounging in his wingback in a way that made my mouth water, his jacket undone, his crisp shirt unbuttoned just enough to let me see a light dusting of chest hair. His chin rested on his fist, and he grinned at me roguishly.

"That's better," he said. "Turn around for me."

My cheeks burned at that. I was on display, and even though I was mostly covered up, I knew that he wanted it this way. Wanted me to feel like he owned me, from my head to my toes, like I would perform for him, for his pleasure, at his say so.

I turned, slowly, my legs shaking, even though I was only in my old flats, my hands clenched into fists. When I turned back around, he was assessing me, an odd, half-grin on his handsome face.

"I like this. It suits you, Lucy. I knew it would."

I looked at the floor, not sure what to say. What did he want me to say? I was being treated like a doll. Like this plaything, and not like an assistant at all. And what's more, the way he was looking at me had relocated my pulse to somewhere between my thighs. This was torture. Did he know how much he was messing with me right now?

Because as much as I might fantasize about a man like Maxwell Pierce, and as much as he might like the idea of fucking me and dumping me, a man like him would never love me, and we both knew it. He would never really want to be with me. And I couldn't afford being my boss' fling. Alex couldn't afford it. And, let's be honest… I'm not sure my heart could, either.

I'd experienced too much loss, too much sadness, and I didn't want it in my love life as well. My high school boyfriend and I had drifted apart, the heartbreak an easy one, but I didn't think I could take this man tearing my heart out of my chest. Not when I'd had him. I couldn't let that happen.

I had to protect myself—my family. I had to be strong.

"There is another uniform I want you to try. The clothing I wish you to wear when you are at home with me."

I nodded and went back into the bathroom without another word. There were a handful of garments at the end of the rack that had been covered by the blouses, and when I found them, I couldn't help the gasp that escaped my mouth. I heard a low chuckle from outside the door, and scowled over my shoulder.

I can't believe this asshole!

I didn't know if the right word was corset or bustier, but either way, I was screwed. There was one in a dark, sensual red, two in black, one white, one pink with a lacy little trim. Added to those were even shorter skirts, the slit going all the way up. He'd see the top of my thigh-highs for sure in those, and if I wasn't careful, everything else.

"Sonofabitch," I muttered under my breath.

Then again… I did sign that contract. And I knew something like this would happen, or at least suspected.

What was it he said that first night?

I heard his voice in my head, then, echoing out of my memory, low and knowing:

"I am a man of particular tastes, and my personal assistant needs to cater to those tastes. Those… needs."

As I tried to figure out a way into the dark red bustier, I cursed myself for being so rash. My fingers shook as I did up the clasps.

"It's not your every day job, to be sure…"

No shit, Mr. Pierce.

"But I think you'll enjoy it."

I let out a bitter laugh, then winced as the boning dug into my ribs. I stood up straight, and the pinching subsided. But when I looked into the mirror, the laughter faded, and I stood stunned, looking at myself in my slitted skirt, breasts pressed in luscious white globes above the rim of the garment, displayed.

Suddenly, the woman in the mirror was no longer little Lucy Willcox, but had been transformed into a graceful courtesan, lusted after by royals and movies stars, kept by billionaires and surrounded with finery, worshipped for her sensuality, her rare beauty, her abandon in the bedroom…

My hair flowed over my shoulder in coppery waves, framing my alabaster skin, rippling over my curves, down to my nipped waist, my milky thighs peeking out from the matching blood-red skirt.

I opened the door to the bathroom as if in a dream, feeling like I was outside of myself—someone else—if only for a little while, floating on the realization that I could be that woman. I could be different. Powerful in my sexuality. Breathtaking.

I saw Mr. Pierce's eyes flit over me, saw his pupils darken as he rose to his feet, heard his breathing grow harsh as he looked me over, examining his handiwork.

"You look ravishing, little Lucy," he breathed.

He reached out and brushed the hair off my shoulders, then he ran his fingers down the long line of my pale throat, as if unable to help himself, trailing down, stopping just before he grazed the swell of my breasts. A line of fire seared my body where his touch had been, my breathing ragged now, my bosom moving in the tight binding fabric.

"Simply ravishing."

He was so close now, his body so near that I could smell his morning coffee and the expensive scent of his cologne. He looked down at me, as if he didn't know what to say, bald lust right there, unhidden in his gaze.

"You need to be punished, you know," he rasped.

"What?"

He turned me around and pressed me to him, my back to his front, holding me tight across my stomach and shoulders, capturing me. I gasped.

"You'll always address me as 'Sir,' when you're being punished, Lucy. Do you understand?"

I nodded frantically, my body heating at his touch, but a cool stab of fear pricking me at the same time. His body was rock hard behind me, and I was tempted to reach down and run my hands over his hard thighs.

"Yes, Sir. I'm sorry, Sir."

"Good," he said, his breath tickling my ear. "You're being punished for not texting me back, Lucy. When I ask you a question on your phone, you will always text back immediately."

"I… "

For a moment, I wasn't sure what he was talking about, but then I remembered.

What part of "immediately" was unclear, Lucy?

This man was absolutely impossible, but as strange as this was, I found myself smiling. He got me again. Damn him.

"I understand, Sir."

"Well, let's just make sure you do," he said.

I stifled a moan as I felt his erection growing, pressing into my backside. He leaned down, then, so close I was sure I would feel his lips on my neck at any moment. I stiffened in his arms, not knowing what I would do if I did. I heard a soft inhale. He was smelling my hair.

Then, his hands were on my shoulders, pushing me across the room toward an ornate end table, and bending me over it.

"Put your arms flat on the table, and don't move until I tell you to."

I placed my forearms on the table, supporting myself on my elbows and risked a glance over my shoulder. Mr. Pierce's eyes were on my backside now, and I bit my lip, realizing he could see the dove gray lace panties peeking out from under that short skirt, and wondering if he liked the view.

I could see his erection tenting his pants, the material tight around what looked like an impressive bulge. My fingers itched to reach back and stroke him through the material, to unzip him and take him out, to feel his hardness in the palm of my hand, but I stayed where I was, obeying him like a good little assistant should.

I can't believe I'm doing this. I can't believe I'm letting this happen again. Is this who I am now? A girl who puts herself on display for her boss?

Mr. Pierce's hands moved under my skirt, and my muscles tensed. What was he about to do? Was he going to violate our contract?

He hiked up the hem until I felt my cheeks bared, but I was still covered by my panties, and he didn't intrude any further.

He paused as if waiting for me to say something, and when I didn't he put one hand on the desk next to me, supporting himself. I almost whimpered, dreading what was coming, but my body already responding, my new panties getting decidedly wetter as the moment stretched, the anticipation pure agony.

When his palm connected with my ass, I made a noise that was half sigh of relief and half shriek. There was a sharp, stinging pain, and then he hit me again, his hand smacking against my other cheek so hard tears burned behind my eyes. The ache stretched out, burning as I waited for another blow to fall. But then he was rubbing me, caressing my cheeks, stroking the pain away.

This was almost worse than the spanking, because I mewled against the table, unable to help myself, arching back into his touch.

Crack!

His hand came down again, making me cry out, the pain redoubled as he hit the bruised flesh, still tender from the other night. Again, his cruel palm landed a blow, then again, and then those dreadful, evil, sweet, wonderful hands were on me again, touching me like no man had ever touched me before, smoothing away the hurt.

My clit was aching, and I realized I was almost painfully turned on. The way he was stroking me, his fingers were just inches from my delicate folds. If I arched a little further, maybe those fingers would slip beneath my panty line, testing my wetness, teasing me, exploring until I cried out beneath him...

His hand came down again and again, and I screamed, my body so tense, I thought I might burst.

"Relax, Lucy," he breathed over me. "Relax, or it will hurt more."

I let the tension out of my muscles as he commanded, and he spanked me again, harder and harder, his blows coming faster now, building almost to a crescendo. I moaned now, the pain changing slowly into something strange—the fuzzy warmth that I'd felt the night before—and a throbbing pleasure flowed through me with each hit, each slap of his strong hands on my ass.

I realized I could hear his ragged breathing, and knew then that he felt as frenzied as I did. I wondered if this is what he did with his other assistants, or if he'd just fucked them from the start, and then his hands were on me again, and all thought became impossible.

He kneaded my ass until I felt tears roll down my cheeks, and then he was holding me, collapsed over me so I could feel that firm cock of his pressed against me once again. I rubbed against it like a cat in heat, and heard him groan in my ear. His length twitched against my ass, making me sting all over again in the most delicious way.

And then, his warmth, his pressure on my back, lifted away.

"That's all for now, Lucy," he said.

I heard the bathroom door slam behind me. I rose up, shaky and feeling tighter wound than a suspension coil. I wanted to cry, I was so goddamn horny, and yet, he was dismissing me yet again.

I straightened my skirt, and left the drawing room, my core aching for him, my heart twinging, my head spinning, wondering what the hell I'd gotten myself into.

A middle aged man in a dark suit knocked on my door an hour later, and bid me change into my office uniform—it was time to go shopping. I nodded, pushing aside my swirling emotions, trying to accept that this was exactly what I'd signed up for. I would wear whatever he wanted me to wear and do whatever he asked, as long as it didn't violate the contract.

I would be at his beck and call, whether I enjoyed this little rollercoaster I was on or not.

Truth be told, my body was still tingling, still unsatisfied even after I'd rubbed myself sore, writhing on the soft linens of my four-poster. It wasn't what I wanted—not even a little bit, and my body knew it as well as my brain.

I went through the motions, knowing I should be enjoying this Pretty Woman moment, being waited on in boutiques finer than I'd ever seen, buying expensive shoes and silk stockings in brands I'd only heard of in the movies. But even Gucci heels couldn't make this afternoon any less strange. Any less confusing.

I wanted my boss. This much I couldn't deny. And to make things worse, it seemed he wanted me. At least his cock sure did. Spanking me got him as hot and hard as it got me soaking wet, but then he didn't act on it. And I didn't want him to, did I?

How wrong would *that* be? I was here to work, and nothing more. I was here for Alex, not for some kinky fling with the man employing me, for heaven's sake!

I almost had a heart attack when the total came up at the cash register, but handed Mr. Pierce's credit card over with trembling hands. He had sent me here, after all, and his butler, Mr. Baker, stood outside, nodding at me encouragingly through the shop window. He had kind eyes, eyes that promised he wasn't messing with me, so I squelched the growing feeling of horror over spending thousands on shoes and took my packages with a smile and a "thank you," in a higher voice than normal.

It was all part of the job, after all. Doing exactly as Mr. Pierce instructed, and nothing less. God help me.

I hadn't seen Mr. Pierce in hours, but I was fully attired now in black hose and garter, along with blood-red hose to match my 'work bustier.' I even dabbed on some rose-colored lipstick I'd brought along, and as I examined myself in the mirror, I felt that same unfamiliar twinge from earlier.

I felt beautiful. No matter how strange the circumstances, I felt sexy for once in my life, and the feeling was intoxicating. It was something I knew I could get used to, if I just gave myself permission.

My phone buzzed next to me, and I snatched it up, not wanting to miss a beat this time.

Meet me in the garage immediately. Bring a notebook.

I flipped through the phone until I found the floor plan I'd been studying, and jogged out the door as quickly as my heels could carry me, snatching up one of many notebooks I'd found in the desk drawer. I'd been exploring, wanting to be on the ball in case he pulled any more of his shenanigans. It was time to get professional all up on his ass and see how he liked it when I refused to play his games.

I made it to the garage in less than two minutes, huffing and puffing in my tight clothing, but prompt nonetheless. It was a large outbuilding in the back of the estate, and my eyes widened as I saw the gleaming, black car raised up on a lift, the sounds of an impact wrench blasting in my ears.

Is that… a Lamborghini?

I'd seen something similar in a Mission Impossible movie and had drooled until I thought I could drool no more, but I'd definitely never seen one in person.

I'd always loved cars, and sometimes helped Buck tune up his truck from time to time for some extra cash. Alex and I had studied at our father's knee before he passed away, although Isabeau had always found it dull work. The smell of grease made me smile as I approached the open doorway.

There was an old picture pinned up on some corkboard that caught my eye. A grainy Polaroid of a smiling man in overalls and two dirty little boys, each holding a wrench up proudly. In front of them was what looked like a soapbox derby car. I reached a hesitant finger out to touch it, but yanked it back as I heard a scraping noise behind me.

Mr. Pierce slid out from under the car on a rolling dolly, wearing a set of ancient-looking coveralls. He slid up his goggles and grinned at me. I smiled at the smear of oil gracing one chiseled cheekbone. I did *not* see this coming.

"Good work, Lucy. That was much a better response time than this morning."

I raised an eyebrow as if to say *I've got your number, Mister.* "Thank you, Sir."

"Now, I wanted to give you my basic schedule and needs for tomorrow at the office. Take this down, please."

The click of my pen echoed through the space, and I flipped the notebook open, ready and waiting for my instructions.

"A car will take you to the office ahead of me. I want you to have my usual breakfast waiting from the café across the street at 9:00 a.m. when I arrive—one whole wheat bagel with cream cheese and a large cappuccino, extra hot."

My pen flew across paper. I didn't want to miss a detail, or I knew he'd redden my backside. Literally. And after the past couple of days, I didn't know if I could deal with that so soon. Not when each time he touched me, I found it harder and harder to control myself. Plus, if I wasn't careful, I wouldn't sit for a week.

Everything in moderation, right?

I allowed myself a secret smile as he continued to speak.

"After that, please go through my email and delete anything not absolutely urgent. I get a lot of people including me in things I have no interest in, and I don't want to see it, understood?"

"Yes, Sir."

"Good. Next, familiarize yourself with my calendar, and call me out of my office for anything important."

"How will I…"

"Next, please get with Nancy in finance so you can assume my payroll sign off duties. After that, I'll give you my order for lunch, which I take at precisely 1 p.m."

I sighed and kept writing. This was insane. How was I supposed to know what he thought was important or not? But I took my notes as he kept on, asking me to call him only in case of such-in-such and fetch coffee for him at whatever specific time of day.

Looking at my notes, I couldn't help but wonder exactly what it was he did at his father's auto corporation except eat and get jacked up on caffeine. I supposed I'd find out soon enough.

"That's all for now, Lucy. I'll be in for dinner. Mrs. O'Doyle serves every night at 8 p.m. sharp, so please don't be late."

I thought of Isabeau's dinner dress, and bit my lip, hovering over him. He looked up from the dolly, an expression of annoyance on his handsome brow.

"What is it, Lucy? Spit it out."

"Should I… should I dress for dinner, Sir?"

He stared at me, then, for a long moment, those piercing blue eyes of his shimmering with amusement.

"You are dressed the way I wish you to dress in my home, Lucy. Any other questions?"

His tone was cold, although his face betrayed him. He loved seeing me off-kilter like this. Loved knowing that I was thinking of appearing in front of his grumpy old housekeeper dressed like his personal escort. Ugh.

"No, Sir. Thank you, Sir."

I turned on my heels and clip-clopped away from him. Away from his beautiful, black car, and his beautiful, mocking eyes. Away from his infuriating "instructions" and his impossible expectations.

I would show him. Tomorrow, he would see that it takes a lot more than that to ruffle little Lucy Willcox. He had no idea who he was dealing with.

When Mr. Pierce arrived at the office at 9 a.m., I was sitting in my work clothes at the large, mahogany desk in front of his door, smiling pleasantly and humming as I worked. I handed him his coffee and bagel and he grinned at me in that wolfish way that told me he couldn't wait until I broke another one of his unspoken rules. I grinned right back.

I'll be the assistant you never knew you wanted but always needed, big boy.

I'd spoken to Mr. Baker and arrived an hour earlier than arranged, taking the time to familiarize myself with my new boss' inbox and meeting schedule before he even knew my car had left the house. I searched through his "deleted" folder and found every meeting request scheduled in the past month neatly stowed there. The only meetings on his schedule were for lunches with investors, and those were few and far between.

Very interesting.

Some quick Googling told me that his father had retired last year, leaving Maxwell Pierce in the coveted CEO position. I also noted that Mr. Pierce's older brother, Jackson, had refused the position in order to pursue a career in politics. It looked like my boss was second pick.

That's gotta hurt, especially coming from the old man.

I thought of the picture I'd seen in the garage, and wondered if I'd caught a glimpse of the two brothers together, laughing with their father. At least they still had a love of cars in common, I supposed. I hoped the company hadn't come between them, but looking through Mr. Pierce's disorganized files, I had a sinking feeling things weren't looking too rosy.

One of the deleted meetings was a recurring one from product development, updating the leadership team on the new line of cars, launching next year. I chewed a pen cap, reading over the including minutes from the past couple of months, before making a decision.

After color coding Mr. Pierce's incoming messages by level of urgency and deleting his spam, I decided to dig a little deeper. I still had an hour before my boss was due to arrive, and as a girl who'd never been afraid of a little hard work, I knew a whole hell of a lot could be accomplished in an hour.

So, when I'd given my boss enough time to enjoy his breakfast and glance nonchalantly at his email, I rapped on his door, thick and intimidating, trimmed with brass, with the words: Maxwell Pierce, CEO centered in the middle.

"Come in."

I took a deep breath, trying to tamp down the nerves threatening to claw their way out of me. My stomach churned, but I knew I was doing the right thing. I had to be. This was the right thing to do. He'd probably thank me.

I hoped.

I pushed the door open, and entered Mr. Pierce's office. The room was brighter than I'd expected, with wide windows all along one wall, and modern photographs of his father's cars supplying pops of color along the others. His feet were up on the desk, expensive leather shoes glowing in the sunlight.

"Yes, Lucy?"

I cleared my throat, which suddenly felt like it had a frog sitting right in the middle of it.

"I… I wanted to remind you about your 11 a.m. meeting, Sir."

"My…?"

"Your 11 a.m. meeting," I said, my voice gaining strength.

I straightened my skirt, my fingers tracing the slit, and stood a little taller.

"As CEO, don't you think you should be involved in the product launch meetings? They recur every Monday at 11 a.m."

His brow furrowed, his intense eyes narrowing as he took in what I'd said. He opened his mouth to protest, but I laid a folder down on his desk with a *thwack*.

"Don't worry, Sir. I've reviewed the minutes and highlighted the various materials you'll need to be abreast of in this outline. I've also taken the liberty of telling the V.P. of Product Development that you'll be reviewing and approving all new product designs going forward."

His frown became alarming then as something flitted behind those eyes. Was that fear I saw? Or something else? On such a powerful man, whatever it was, it was deeply unsettling.

Oh, God. I should have minded my own business. Good fucking work, Lucy!

I sensed it, then. I was going to be fired, and Alex was going to be hurt, maybe killed, all because I had to stick my nose into this man's business. Why did I care what he did with his father's company? Why did I want him to excel? Wasn't I getting paid either way?

God damn!

"Thank you, Lucy," he said, his voice so low I almost couldn't hear him. "That will be all for now."

I pressed my lips together and backed away, toward the door. As I gripped the knob, his voice made me freeze in my tracks.

"We *will* talk about this tonight. Mark my words."

I swallowed hard. "Yes, Sir."

I left the office as fast as my tight skirt would let me, closing the door carefully behind me.

* * *

Come see me in the master suite immediately. We have a lot to talk about, little Lucy.

I hate to say it, but I was truly afraid walking down that hall for the first time since I met Mr. Pierce. Sure, there had been anxiety when I was signing the contract, and some good-old-fashioned wariness when he'd bent me over his knee, but nothing like this. This was real fear, pure and simple.

Mr. Pierce was going to fire me. I'd failed so quickly. And all because I couldn't mind my own damn business.

When I raised my fist to knock on his door, it opened so fast I almost fell into his arms. I caught myself, stumbling and correcting, and reared back at the look in his eyes. They were almost black, his look so passionate, so angry, so fiery, I almost couldn't meet his gaze.

"Get in here," he growled.

He slammed the door behind me, and turned on me like an animal cornering his prey. I backed up until my rump hit the edge of his tall mattress.

"Please, Sir," I said, but he held up his hand, shutting me up as quickly as if he'd slapped me.

"What do you think you're doing? Meddling in things you don't understand? Huh? Answer me!"

He moved toward me until he was towering over me, his chest heaving with emotion.

"Just who do you think you are?"

"Y-you're assistant," I whispered. "Your assistant, Sir."

"I don't remember asking you to get involved in my work life, Lucy. I remember asking you to sign off on payroll and *get my fucking lunch.* That's all!"

I kept silent, my heartbeat in my throat, as he paced before me.

"Well? Do you remember me asking you to change my fucking schedule? To get me involved in any projects?"

He stopped in front of me and tilted my chin up so I'd meet his gaze. "Do you?"

"No, Sir," I breathed.

I wanted to look away, but some instinct kept my grey eyes on his. There was rage in his eyes, but also something else. Something inscrutable. Something that made my blood heat to look at it. Something fierce and primal and utterly fascinating.

"Then why did you do that, Lucy?"

His voice was low now, challenging. Threatening.

"Because you needed it, Sir. You're worth more than you think."

I don't know why I said it, but there it was. He wasn't just some sloppy seconds, reluctantly place holding for his brother. He was smart and resourceful. Hell, he practically oozed leadership.

"What?" he spat.

"It's just... it's a waste! You're so much better than that..."

He held my chin hard, his fingers pressing into my face. "How do *you* know?"

I looked back, returning his gaze, tears pricking the backs of my eyes.

"I just do."

He bared his teeth for a moment, his rage just at the surface, and then he did something I didn't expect at all when I walked through his door. He kissed me hard, his lips electric on mine, making my mind go blank, and my toes curl inside my shoes. When he released my chin, he stepped back, looking just as shocked as I felt.

"Lucy, I... I'm sorry. Our contract-"

But before he could say anything more, I grabbed his tie and pulled him to me, kissing him again before the moment could end, before the spell broke and he kicked me out of his life.

I felt something snap between us, an almost audible crackle as the last piece of resistance crumbled away, and then he was holding me, crushing me to him until he stole my breath away.

His lips on mine were heart-breakingly soft, but his tongue darting into my mouth, parting my lips and making melt against him, was all lust, all heat. I tasted him in return, sighing as I ran my tongue over his, our breath mingling as we came together.

Strong hands roamed over my curves, savoring my small waist before grabbing my ass hard in a way that made my whole body throb. I fumbled with his tie before jerking it off his neck and starting on his buttons, but then he was pushing my hands way and ripped it open carelessly, the fabric tearing in his haste to get undressed for me.

One rough tug, and my bodice was half-open, the hooks-and-eyes popping under pressure. He growled in frustration and tore the rest wide apart, and I gasped as my nipples hit the cool air of the bedroom. His eyes traveled over me, his mouth curling into that dangerous grin of his, but before I could feel any sort of shyness or think about covering myself, he bent down and suckled first one peak into his mouth, then the other, drawing on me roughly.

I moaned breathlessly and threw my head back, my hair tickling my naked back. When he bit my nipple, I cried out, that familiar twinge of painful pleasure making me ache for him. I twisted my fingers through his thick, dark hair, loving the way he was suckling, teasing, biting, driving me absolutely wild.

I slid a hand between us and jerked at his buckle. His hot lips made their way up to my neck, licking me in a way that made my feet flex and my cheeks flush. He was so hot, so amazingly oh-my-God on fire, I couldn't believe this was really happening.

But it was. It was happening to *me*.

He didn't bother with my skirt, but just pushed the slits up over my slender hips and tore at my underwear, ripping it off my body with a shredding sound that made me wince. But when I reached between us and felt his hot, silky hardness in my palm, I forgot all about the price tag of those fancy duds. All that mattered was this moment, here with him.

He pushed my thighs back roughly, spreading me open for him, his hands brushing over the garters, making me tingle.

He leaned down, smelling me, and I covered my mouth, wanting to say 'stop, no, wait,' but somehow no words came out.

"You smell good enough to eat," he said, and lowered his mouth to my aching folds.

His tongue darted out, and I arched my back, groaning at the over-the-moon amazing feeling of him tasting me there. He lapped at me, holding my legs open firmly, and I heard him moan as well, laving and teasing my needy body.

"You taste so sweet, little Lucy… So goddamn sweet."

I tugged at his hair, breathless and squirming as he laved me again and again. I'd never had a man do this before, never even had one offer, and the idea that my gorgeous boss was loving me like this, *savoring me*, even, made me feel light-headed.

When he bit my clit, I screamed, writhing on the bedclothes, my pleasure reaching a delicate plateau. But it was his fingers testing me, spreading me, then plunging deeply inside of my wetness that sent me over the edge. I shuddered, my thighs trembling in his grip as I came around him, squeezing him again and again until I heard him utter a reverant "*Fuck.*"

Mr. Pierce rose up from between my thighs, his face shining with my arousal, and I stared at him with half-lidded eyes, panting, my body still convulsing around his fingers. He drew them out and offered them to me, and I took them without question, suckling them between my lips, tasting the musky-sweetness of my cum, and knowing that he had just tasted the same.

His lips met mine again, and we shared the taste of my ecstasy, our tongues gliding over one another, my core hot, my body electric, and not at all sated yet. When we broke apart, Mr. Pierce's eyes were full of wonder—a wonder that I shared completely.

"God, Lucy," he growled.

He grabbed a fistful of my hair, and I moaned as he tugged it, asserting his control.

"I'm going to fuck you so hard," he said. "So *fucking hard.* Now, get on your knees."

I did as he commanded, turning around on my knees for him, my whole body practically vibrating with anticipation. I wanted him. *Needed* him so badly, I could cry. When he pressed me down so my head hit the pillows and my ass stuck up in the air, I didn't resist. Instead I arched my back, urging him on, my fists clutching the sheets, bracing for him.

I felt the thick head of his shaft pressing at my entrance and whimpered beneath him. He pulled back, and I felt his fingers inside of me once again, sliding through my slickness, and then he was pressing again, his tip lubricated with my slickness. He pushed forward then, and I gasped as I felt his girth slip inside of me.

He was large, and I felt a twinge of pain as my small body adjusted to the feel of him there, filling me. But before I could relax, he slammed inside of me in one sharp thrust. I gave a hitching moan, and heard him grunt behind me.

"You're so tight, little Lucy."

His fingers dug into my hips as he began moving in earnest, sliding in and out of me slowly at first, then picking up the pace as I mewled beneath him, my channel alight with the sweet friction of our coupling. I felt the heavy slap of his balls against my folds, each movement, each feel of skin against skin making my toes curl. When he released one hip from his grasp and slapped my sore ass, I screamed.

"That's right," he said. "Take what I have to give you."

He wound his fist into my hair again, and gave it a sharp yank as he thrust faster, pounding into me. The way he controlled me, the way he held me tight, riding me harder, even as he pressed me down, made me feel wanton and wild in a way I'd never felt before.

He reached around my waist and slapped at my pussy in short, sharp motions, the end of his fingers hitting my sensitive clit.

"Cum for me, Lucy. Cum for your master…"

Hearing his words, his demand that I fall apart in his arms once again, I felt my pleasure spilling over, and heard the scream rip from my throat. He pinched my clit once as I came, the spike of delicious stinging making my entire body shake with the force of my orgasm.

One hand around my waist, and one still fisted in my hair, he drew my back up to meet his chest, holding me close as he pistoned in and out of me mercilessly, driving into me over and over until I wondered how much more of him I could take. I squeezed around him, milking him, willing him to cum inside of me, to make me his.

With a final thrust, he stiffened behind me, holding me close, his lips on my neck, and I felt him inside of me, spilling his hot seed. I pushed back against him, grinding onto him, wanting every bit that he had to offer.

We stayed together, panting, moving gently, him running his hands lazily over my breasts, and my hands wandering over the hard planes of his thighs. When we finally broke apart, he collapsed on the bed, his erection still stiff and proud. I gazed at it with wide eyes, that beautiful cock that had just been inside of me, and ran my hand over it curiously, appreciating its length and thickness.

God, this man was something else.

He pulled me down next to him, then, wrapping his arms around me so my head lay on his chest and placed a soft kiss on my hair. We lay there for some time, neither speaking, but comfortable in the silence. When I thought he may have fallen asleep, I felt him stir beneath me.

"Lucy... about the contract. Our arrangement..."

I frowned and buried my head against his hard body. Was he going to call it off? After what we'd just done? What we'd just shared? Was I that big of an idiot after all?

"If you don't want things to be this way going forward, I'll understand. Your job is not in jeopardy."

I sighed against him, smiling where he couldn't see. "And if I do want it... if I *do* want it to be this way?"

He rolled over on his side, propping himself up on one elbow. His blue eyes held mine, and I saw the wicked glint there before he gave me his lopsided grin.

"Then I'm going to have to teach you my rules."

"Rules?"

"Yes, little Lucy. If you're going to be with me like this, I will have to train you. And you'll have to agree to me being your master... at least when we're in the bedroom."

Master...

He'd used that word when he told me to cum for him, when he'd commanded my body, and I'd done what he'd told me with more pleasure than I'd ever felt with a man before. He'd *felt* like my master, then. Felt like he owned me. And what was stranger, I felt safe that way. Comforted. Taken care of.

Almost loved.

"And what would I be if I let you be my master, Sir?"

He chuckled at my use of 'Sir,' and lightly stroked my hip beneath my bunched-up skirt.

"You'd be my slave, of course," he said.

I fell back on the pillow, staring at him, emotions mixing in my mind until I couldn't tell if I was frightened or titillated—or, let's face it, a little bit of both--at the thought.

"You'd be my slave, but that means I would take care of you. You obey me when we're together like this, when you're in my bed, and in return, I'll take you places you've never even dreamed of."

He leaned over and gripped my ass, making me screech as he pressed into the bruises there.

"Do you like that? Did you like that when I gave you that little edge of pain? Of discipline?"

I moaned as he squeezed me again, the sensation shooting straight to my core. Yes, I most certainly *did* like it. I really, really did, much to my own surprise.

"Yes, Sir."

"Well, that's not all I will give you. I'll bind you. Blindfold you. Take your trust to the limits. Do you want that, Lucy? Do you want to trust me like that?"

Thoughts of being handcuffed by him, of him taking me while I was tied to his bedposts, of doing unmentionable things to me when I was vulnerable before him, made my pussy clench. I reached my hand up and toyed with a dark curl that had fallen down over his forehead.

"Yes, Sir. I do."

"Excellent," he said, grinning like the cat who just caught a mouse. "Then your training begins tomorrow. In the office."

He rolled over on his side, away from me, leaving me lying there, still in my skirt, hose and heels.

"Sir?"

"Goodnight, Lucy," he said, yawning. "You'd better get some rest. Tomorrow's a big day, after all."

He reached over to his side table and clicked off the lamp. Darkness fell over the room. I lay back on the pillows, not quite knowing what to think or if he wanted me there with him in his room or if I'd been dismissed once again.

I was just about to get up and start groping for my things, when I heard him chuckle again next to me. His hand grabbed mine in the darkness, and he pulled me to his side.

Dear God, but this man was insufferable.

And, why, oh, why did I love that so much?

Chapter Three

Lucy

"Come see me in my office."

Who knew six little words could hold such power? That six little words could make me shiver from head to toe, excitement coursing through me like a drug? When the intercom buzzed beside me, I felt my muscles tense, my whole body tingling, ready for whatever my dominant boss had to give me.

I pressed the button with a red lacquered nail. I'd dressed as he instructed, in an expensive red silk top tucked into a high-waisted black pencil skirt, my red curls done up in a loose French twist. Every bit the sexy assistant he wanted me to be.

"Right away, Sir."

My breathing was heavy, my voice higher than normal as I answered him. I imagined I could hear his low chuckle through the heavy wooden door behind me, but I knew that was impossible. I felt his presence behind me, so large it seemed like he was the only one in the office, filling the space with his power. His magnetism.

I rapped on his door, suddenly nervous, shifting on my Louboutin heels. Mr. Pierce said last night that he'd begin training me today, but what exactly did that mean? Was he going to spank me again, right here in the office, or was there more in store today for little Lucy Willcox, now Sexy Lucy, the Executive Assistant?

"Come in."

His voice sent a shiver down my spine. I pushed the door open and entered, then closed it soundly behind me. Mr. Pierce was behind his desk, his fingers tented beneath his chin, watching me with a half smile, his blue eyes glittering with mischief.

"We need to establish some ground rules, Lucy, if you're going to be with me."

If I'm going to be your slave, you mean.

The thought almost made moan aloud, remembering the way he'd taken me last night, making me fall apart in his arms.

"Yes, Sir."

He smirked and sat back, assessing me his hungry gaze.

"First, when we are playing together, or when you're being punished, you will always address me like you just did. You may call me 'Sir' or 'Master,' but nothing else."

I nodded, a little tingle shooting straight down to that naughty spot between my legs that always seemed to betray me when this man was around. I knew it should feel weird calling him my master, calling him Sir while he called me Lucy or Slave or God-only-knows-what, but when I thought about it, I felt only excitement. Excitement about being in his hands, totally under his control, at least for those brief moments.

With everything on my mind, Alex in trouble, Isabeau probably hurt and angry, losing control definitely had its appeal.

"Next, I expect you to follow my schedule exactly. I *hate* surprises, Lucy. Understood?"

"Yes, Sir."

Man, was this guy uptight. You'd think a man like Maxwell Pierce could handle a little twist or two in life, but he really did like everything on his terms and his terms only. Was there a personality type above Type A in terms of being a total control freak? Type Alpha, maybe?

Mr. Pierce stood and moved around the desk like a wolf stalking his prey. He stood before me and tilted my chin up, forcing me to meet his eyes.

"If you really understood, Lucy, you wouldn't have booked that meeting for me this morning with R&D."

I felt my cheeks heating.

Oh, right. That.

I'd put a reminder on his calendar for 10:00 a.m., despite his previous objections. I was deadly serious about him being more involved in his own company, and since he didn't exactly fire me last time I butted in…

"Good thing I have an assistant who can attend for me."

"Attend *for* you, Sir?"

"That's right." He grinned down at me, his finger now tracing my jaw, his touch making me shiver. "You're going to be punished, little miss Lucy. You will attend the meeting in my place and take detailed notes for me, then brief me later today. Understood?"

I sighed. "Yes… Sir."

Goddamn him. This is not at all what I wanted. But at least he was getting involved, in his own weird way. I supposed that was better than nothing.

"Good girl," he said.

He gathered up the bottom of my skirt, and I gasped, looking over my shoulder toward the office door.

"Don't worry, Lucy. No one comes to see me who isn't scheduled in by my assistants. It's a hard and fast rule I've set with my employees."

He moved closer, pulling me against his body. I instinctively slid my hands up his chest, enjoying the muscles beneath. His lips met my neck, and I moaned. He cupped my ass, then slid his hands beneath the fabric, running his hands over my thin panties and garter belt.

I was already wet for him, my body responding to his presence even before his touch. When he slipped a finger beneath my panties, I opened wider for him, pressing into him, loving the way he grew stiff against my belly.

"You're already soaking, you bad girl."

His breath tickled my neck as I leaned against him, supported by him, as he explored my folds, sending little jolts of electricity through my body. My core was on fire for him, and I wondered if he would take me here and now--wished it with all of my being.

Would he bend me over the desk? Would he press me against the wall? Would he take me on the floor, rubbing my still-sore ass against the rough fibers of the carpet?

He reached into his pocket and drew something out, but before I could see what it was, I felt it pressed against me, inside of the lace of my underwear, its cool, rounded surface totally foreign. Mr. Pierce reached into his pocket again, and the object buzzed to life against me. I shrieked, squirming in his arms.

"Open your legs, Lucy."

I pressed my lips together, mewling in protest, but did as my master commanded. He slipped the egg-shaped toy inside of me, my body stretching around it, clenching and unclenching as it *buzz, buzz, buzzed*, making me feel like my head may explode at any moment.

Either that, or I'd have a screaming orgasm right here in the office, courtesy of Mr. Pierce's evil little toy.

"Don't you *dare* cum, Lucy. I haven't given you my permission."

I looked up at him, my eyes pleading. He grinned back, unmoved.

"That's my third rule, my dear little slave. You will only cum when I tell you to. I own your pleasure, Lucy. It's mine, just like you are mine."

I nodded, tears stinging my eyes as I squeezed the egg inside of me. The vibrations were too much—too intense.

I thought of doing my taxes. Thought of how much I hated it when I'd just smoothed my hair down and it was raining outside. Fixed my thoughts on the smell of dirty coins, rotten bananas and my grandmother's floral perfume.

Just when I thought I might fall apart anyway, despite it all, the buzzing stopped.

Sweet, merciful Zeus!

I panted, holding on to my boss's expensive suit sleeve, trying not to look at his laughing eyes.

"Good girl," he said.

He pressed a kiss to the top of my head and backed away, holding me at arms' length.

"Now, I'm going be listening the whole time."

He handed me what looked like a blue tooth headset, which I slipped on, frowning.

What kind of fucked up game was this?

"I can hear and speak to you through this piece. I have the remote control to my special toy and can activate it at any time. I trust you'll be professional and take notes as I requested. I'll know if you're misbehaving, Lucy," he said.

He tapped my lip, and I wrinkled my nose at him.

"Don't let me down."

I chewed my lip where he'd touched me, staring up at him. He couldn't be serious. Could he? The look on his face brooked no argument.

"You are one sick dude, Sir," I said.

He laughed, the sound making me tingle all over again, then leaned in until his face was only an inch from mine.

"This is your punishment for surprising me. Remember that."

I shook hands with the engineers and the director of product development, all men, I couldn't help but notice, and introduced myself, making my apologies for my boss being absent.

"He's working on a project he can't tear himself away from," I said.

A low chuckle sounded in my ear, and I jumped. One of the engineers, Brad, gave me a funny look.

"Just got a little static shock," I said.

My face grew hot again, but I pressed my lips together, smoothed my skirt down, and resolved to make the best of things. After all, what choice did I have?

"You're right, you know," his voice said in my ear. "I find you very difficult to tear myself away from, Lucy."

At that moment, the egg roared to life--silent, but making me shift in my chair like I'd just been goosed.

The director began his team's presentation, introducing who was working on what aspect of the new car's design. I whimpered softly, riding the wave of electric pleasure pulsing and buzzing and tingling, driving me to distraction.

I opened my laptop and began click-clacking away, typing notes along with the thoughts popping into my head.

Brad is working on electrical work for the console, and Steve thinks that part of the project will be ready to show in three weeks.

You son of a bitch. This is waaaaay too far!

There will be a follow up meeting next week to go over the steering column. Andy will head that up.

If I live through this, I'm going to spank YOU for a change, you pompous, arrogant...

The egg went still. My body still squeezed around it, and I shivered, trying desperately to back away from that precipice. I couldn't cum in the middle of a meeting!

Especially because you don't have his permission, the little voice in my head helpfully supplied.

"You're doing very well, little Lucy."

His voice was a low rumble in my ear. I squeezed my thighs together hard, hating him. Wanting him.

I imagined for one moment what this must be like for him. Was he touching himself, knowing what he was doing to me?

I shook my head and started typing again. I needed to focus, or I'd be well and truly screwed. He really did need this information, after all. This wasn't just some sicko sexual game. This was his life! And I knew he needed to grab the bull by the horns instead of being some billionaire spectator, watching his opportunities pass him by.

He was better than that, even if he didn't see it. I believed in him.

After all, no one could be that sadistic without also being wildly creative.

I smirked at the thought, then bit my tongue as the egg buzzed again, this time pulsing, on off, on off, on off.

That low laugh again. Oh, he must just be *loving* this.

"Your face is beautiful when you blush, Lucy," he said.

I looked up in surprise, then narrowed my eyes as I noticed the web camera pointing right at me at the top of the laptop. He'd been watching me the whole time.

What an *ass*.

I did my best to ignore him, even as he started pulsing the egg in new patterns inside of me, making my body heat and my blood boil. My core actually *ached*, shuddering with need, held right on the edge of orgasm until I thought I might pass out from the effort. The self control.

Sweat trickled down my lower back until it rested on the band of my skirt. I cleared my throat, shifting in my chair until the presenter stopped mid-sentence and looked right at me.

"Are you alright, Lucy?"

"Yep! Yes. Just… allergies."

I grabbed a kleenex from the middle of the table and made a show of blowing my nose.

"Spring's a bitch, am I right?"

A few men nodded, then looked back at the PowerPoint.

"Cum for me now, little Lucy," whispered Mr. Pierce. "Cum now."

I typed frantically now, both notes and nonsense, all of it mixing together, but I needed to move some part of my body, or I thought I might die, right then and there. My molecules would fly apart like in a bad science fiction movie, and I'd be scattered across the room, across the building, across time and space, floating aimlessly, hopelessly apart from all other pieces of myself, never to recover.

My fingers shook as I came for him—my boss. My master. My devious Mr. Pierce.

Production is scheduled for XJKFSkaskaspaodsiaskLDF:Fndkfaplsl;has!

My heel tapped against the carpet, my foot arching in my shoe as waves of pulsing, white-hot pleasure ripped through me, making me think of one thing—Mr. Pierce's hungry blue eyes, watching me, watching my face, knowing I'd done as he commanded, even if no one else did.

There was a sigh in my ear, almost like he was right there with me, then his voice.

"Very good. Very, very good job, Lucy…"

I was sweating all over when I finally escaped the meeting room.

When I rapped on his office door, he jerked it open immediately, like he'd been waiting on the other side for me to come to him.

"Come," he said.

I did, closing the door behind me. He yanked me over to the desk and bent me over it without saying a word, breathing hard, seeming as ragged and needy as I was. Maybe even more so.

"Do you want this, Lucy?" His voice was a growl. "Do you want me to fuck you raw now that you've been punished?"

"Yes," I said. "Goddamit, *yes.*"

He shoved my skirt up and jerked my panties so hard that the lace tore. He threw them across the room, then gently worked the egg out of my body and tossed it aside. Then, two of his fingers worked inside of me, making me moan, my lips against his desk.

I turned my head and watched him grip his erection, rubbing my juices across the head and shaft, before grabbing my ass and spreading me open for him. When he thrust into me, the whole desk rocked, scooting a half-inch across the floor.

I cried out, my body screaming its approval at finally being filled. I reached back to touch him, but he grabbed my hands and slapped them on the desk.

"No you don't, slave. This is my time. And I will take you how I please. Hands flat on the desk."

"Yes… Sir…" I said between thrusts, my channel squeezing him, already begging for release.

His hand came down on my ass, and I shrieked, grateful for the sturdiness of the wooden door, praying this office was soundproof. Mr. Pierce did nothing to shut me up, so that was probably a good sign. Because I really didn't think I could help myself even if it wasn't.

"I want to use this tight little body of yours, Lucy."

His hand slapped down again, stinging the same spot. I could practically feel each fingerprint glowing red on the white skin of my ass, and grinned against the desk, loving that he was marking me as he took me, fucking me like he took for granted that I was his.

"I want you to understand who your master is…"

He spanked me again and again, drawing moans from me, making my breath hiss through my teeth from the stinging, burning pleasure welling up in me with each stroke of his thick shaft, each swat of his palm on my tender flesh.

I arched my back, feeling him deeper, pounding a place inside of me no man had reached before. My fingers curled into claws on the desk, and I realized I was panting with the effort of not coming apart until he told me to. Until he gave me permission.

The thought frightened me as much as it thrilled me.

I was his, already his, despite my fear.

"Who's your master, Lucy?"

"You are…"

He spanked me again, this time with bruising force. "Who?"

"You are! Sir!"

He massaged my aching cheeks, and I whimpered beneath him.

"Don't you forget it, girl."

He pulled me up, then, holding me as my back arched, fucking me harder, my thighs banging against his desk as he took me, each thrust making me ache deep inside, longing to cum with him, to please him, to make him mine as I was his.

His hand held my throat, the other holding me firmly around my waist, pulling me back onto him with each stroke. I wailed now, my head falling back, trusting him to hold me, to keep me safe even as he took me like an animal, right here in his office.

I could smell the mingling scent of our sex, the spice of his cologne surrounding me, the sound of skin slapping skin filling my ears.

"Cum, little Lucy," he said.

Both hands moved to my breasts, squeezing hard, and I did as he commanded, gasping as I came apart, my body trembling as he rode me, his thumbs tracing the hard peaks of my nipples. When he pulled me tight to his chest, I heard his ragged sigh, and knew he'd found his completion inside of me.

He ground lazily against me, trailing kisses down my neck. I leaned back, wrapping my hand in his hair, loving the feeling of just being still with him, his cock stiff inside of me. When he slid out, I sighed at the empty feeling, my pussy aching in a way that made me smile.

"That… will be all for now, Lucy."

I straightened my skirt, flattened my blouse, and left the office like a professional, grinning all the way.

When I left for the night, instead of the car that brought me into the office waiting, lower headlights flashed, and a roar filled my ears as a black shape rolled toward me.

The Lamborghini…

That car made my mouth water and my palms sweat. I wanted to run my hands across its sleek lines, and would probably go straight to Heaven if I got the opportunity to get under that sexy hood and tinker around. It was love at first sight, and seeing it again, I smiled like an idiot.

The door slid upward and I groaned with envy. What a sweet, sweet ride. This billionaire better appreciate what he had, or he was going to get a real earful.

"Going my way?"

Mr. Pierce grinned from behind the steering wheel, looking mouth-watering himself with his jacket off and his crisp, white sleeves rolled up, tie loose and dangling. He looked like he fell out of a GQ catalog, and I couldn't help but shake my head as I slid into the cool, leather seat.

"You know I am, Sir."

I snapped the door shut and buckled up, admiring the smooth contours of the console. God, this was a gorgeous car.

"I have something to show you."

He brushed my hair away from my shoulders, and I shivered at his touch.

"Do you trust me, Lucy?"

I smiled at him. Despite his wild side, and his petulant bad-boy attitude at work, I felt his strength, his kindness. I knew he was a good man. Maybe even a great one.

"Yes, Sir."

He nodded in the darkness, those intense eyes of him glinting from the blue lights on the dash.

"Then, hold on tight."

He peeled out of the parking lot and drove up a side street, doing no more than five over the speed limit, but giving me a taste of what this car could do with his swift acceleration. Where was he taking me in a car like this? I knew it was no good for city driving, so why had he picked me up like this?

We drove in silence for a while, and I noticed we were leaving the city lights behind us, pulling into a stretch of highway leading to the straight lines of the dark country roads. I had only been in the city here, so far away from home, and hadn't been expecting this lonely stretch of road. What the hell did he have planned?

Suddenly, Mr. Pierce veered onto a side road, the car swinging off the highway and onto a narrow one-lane strip of pavement. It wandered through the trees and shrubs, and soon, the highway was lost behind us. I was about to ask what was going on, when I saw headlights coming up ahead of us like fireflies on a summer night.

"This used to be an old airfield," he said. "Now, its just abandoned strips of pavement with no one to use them. Sometimes a few buddies and I get together and drive here. It seems like a shame to waste good asphalt."

He grinned in the darkness, his eyes glinting.

"Ready to take the ride of your life?"

I stared, open-mouthed, my knuckles whitening as I gripped the edge of my seat.

"Am I?"

Mr. Pierce revved the engine and chuckled. "Hold on tight, little Lucy. Things are about to get wild."

Isabeau

I sat in the dark pool hall, nursing a beer, my husband beside me drinking a scotch and soda. The clack of billiard balls and the grumbling of gambling men surrounded us, but all I could think about was the time. According to the Budweiser clock over the bar, it was two minutes to 3 p.m.

And at 3 p.m., the private detective we hired would arrive to tell us what he'd found out about the man named Dmitry. The man who threatened to kill my brother. The man who was now extorting my sister. The man who had to be dealt with fast or my family would fall apart around me.

Mr. Drake squeezed my leg under the table, and I looked up into his eyes. He smiled at me, and I felt some of the tension in my shoulders loosen, if only for a moment.

"It will be alright, Isa. He should be here soon."

At that moment, the door squealed open, sunlight splashing the floor as a man entered the bar. He was middle aged and balding, with a comb-over that wasn't hiding anything.

The unnerved part of my brain wanted to laugh. What good could a man be at discovering people's secrets when he hid his own so badly?

He nodded at Mr. Drake and slid into the booth across from us. He raised a finger toward the bar.

"My usual, Tony."

There was a grunting reply, and he turned to us, folding his hands on the sticky tabletop.

"I found the guy," he said. "But he's good. Looks clean from the outside. No criminal record, no tax evasion, no nothing. He owns an auto body shop in the center of town and hires ex-cons through some kind of work program. Looks like a friggin' saint, helping out the community."

I leaned forward, my palms sweating against my bottle of beer. "That's it?"

The man looked from Mr. Drake back to me and raised an eyebrow.

"Don't worry, sweet cheeks. For the money you're payin', I'll find a way to get inside and sniff around."

Mr. Drake tensed beside me, his eyes suddenly cold. "You'll refer to my wife as Mrs. Drake or Ma'am *only*, Barry. Do I make myself clear?"

The ferrety man across from us cleared his throat. The bar man came over with a pint of stout and backed away in a hurry at the look in my husband's eyes.

"Crystal," he said. "Apologies, Mrs. Drake."

I kneed Mr. Drake lightly under the table, but was smiling on the inside. He knew I could take care of myself, but the thought of him being so protective was a sweet one.

"Then tell us what you're planning on doing for us, since, like you said, we're paying so well." I smiled and took a swig of my beer.

The man cleared his throat again, his eyes darting from one of us to the other.

"I got a guy. I can get him inside and poking around. I'll get you what you need."

I exchanged a look with Mr. Drake, and he squeezed my hand.

"Barry, if we can't go to the police, we're prepared to pay him off. We just want this to go away as quickly as possible."

"That's okay, too, Mr. D. My guy can get the information on the debt and get back to us with this scumbag's terms."

"Thank you," I said. "Thank you so much. But please hurry. My brother's life is on the line here."

Barry chugged the rest of his beer, tipped his hat and slid out of the booth.

"No worries, Mrs. Drake. Let me take care of things."

He left, and I sunk down in my seat, sighing.

"It will all be fine, Isa. I promise you that."

I leaned my head on my husband's sturdy shoulder, trying to believe his words, that everything would be alright, but feeling only the tension coiling in my stomach at the thought of paying off a piece of dirt like Dmitry.

"I'm sorry…"

"Hush," he said. He slid an arm around me and held me close, his warmth and presence more reassuring than any words he could utter. "I'd to anything for you, Isa. This is nothing but a bump in the road. We'll deal with it together."

I nodded, leaned into him, and listened to the racing beat of my heart.

Lucy

The car idled on the end of a strip of runway stretching away into shadow. A whooping came from the car to our left, and Mr. Pierce leaned out his window.

"You ready to give up that ride, Max?" A blonde man with spikey hair revved his blue Aston Martin beside us.

"You first, Blaine," he said. "Your mom buy you this one, too?" He waggled his finger at him. "She's going to be very disappointed when it's sitting in my drive way, young man."

The blonde man's face fell into a sneer. "Fuck you."

Mr. Pierce shrugged and gave me a wink. "Some people just can't be civil under pressure."

I was still gripping the seat, my mind struggling to accept what was about to happen.

"What's at the end of the runway?"

My voice was too high, my throat tight.

"Oh, it just ends in a rocky field. It'll tear up the suspension in no time flat."

I rolled my eyes up, trying not to freak out. What the hell had I gotten myself into?

"So, let me get this straight, *Sir*," I said. "You're seriously going to drag race the douchebag in the car that costs more than a house, toward a rocky nightmare, in some game of billionaire playboy chicken?"

Mr. Pierce's eyes flashed, but he grinned and gave my upper thigh a squeeze.

"That's why I asked if you trusted me, Lucy. I don't intend to lose."

"But if you do... and you either stop first or screw up this car..."

I had to stop for a moment and close my eyes. The thought of rough gravel digging into the bottom of the Lamborghini was like thinking about someone defacing the Mona Lisa.

"He gets the car, right?"

"Correct. We play for slips."

I rolled my eyes. Of course. Because a quarter million dollar car is a reasonable bet to men like Maxwell.

"Then how, *Sir*, do you expect us to get home?"

Mr. Pierce laughed. "I'll call a cab. But trust me, little Lucy. I never lose."

Another young man with his arms draped over two scantily-clad women walked up beside the cars, looking cool in a silk jacket over jeans. He whispered something to the dark haired beauty on his left, and she covered her mouth, giggling. He turned toward the drivers, his eyes full of raw anticipation.

"Both drivers ready?"

The blonde man whooped like an asshole and Mr. Pierce stuck a hand out the window, signaling with one finger.

"Miko, my dear, do your thing," the man in the jacket said.

The giggling woman moved to the middle of the runway, standing with her arms raised between the two cars, grinning from ear to ear. Her black dress rode up, exposing a sliver of red panty beneath.

"San!"

Mr. Pierce's eyes focused on the road, and I could almost see him blocking out the other driver, who was now yelling taunts through his open windows.

"Ni!"

"Oh God," I said.

Mr. Pierce's lips twitched into a smirk and his hands tightened on the wheel.

"Ichi!"

I tested my seat belt, adjusting it tight across my lap. I realized I *did* trust Mr. Pierce no matter how insane this was, but it never hurt to be safe.

"Itti!"

Miko's hands cut through the air like swords, and the cars roared to life. Tires squealed on the pavement, white smoke billowing out behind, and I covered my hand with my mouth as we sped by, so close to the girl that the tassels on her short skirt whipped around her. She was squealing with delight, her voice matching the sound of the tires eating up the runway.

I felt a jerk somewhere behind my navel as we accelerated, and screamed, but it was not out of fear, but something between fear and joy—a fierce feeling like getting to the top of a rollercoaster, and feeling the world drop out from beneath you as you float for that tiny space of a second, before gravity takes over and you're rushing down, down, down.

"She can get up to 60 in 2.9 seconds," Mr. Pierce said beside me, grinning like a madman. "There's nothing on earth like a V12 in the hands of engineers who know they're doing."

I had to agree.

The Aston Martin was a second behind us, but soon gained, engine roaring as we leveled out.

"Hang on, little Lucy!"

He slowed for a briefest of moments, his leather shoe lifting off the accelerator, and then he downshifted, jerking the wheel to the left. We slid, cornering before I even knew what was happening, my body pressing hard against my door as gravity shifted.

I cried out as the tires caught and we whipped onto a new runway, driving at a 90 degree angle away from the first.

The Aston Martin tore up the pavement behind us, gaining until its front tires were just behind ours. Another breath, another moment, and it would pull ahead.

"I thought you said this was a drag race!"

"Well, we made our own kind of track. Sort of like a maze in here, but it gets the job done. The rocks are at the end. Two more turns and we're there."

Mr. Pierce's eyes were glued to the road, but his face lit up in the darkness, the energy radiating off him like sheet lighting crackling over the fields of my hometown. He was dangerous, all right. Dangerous and wild and completely irresistible.

Hesitantly, I touched his leg. He glanced over at me once, grinning, then those intense, blue eyes of his were on the dark road ahead, minding the car eating up the road beside him.

"Here comes another," he said.

He decelerated, shifted, and coasted around to the right. The Aston Martin hit my side of the car, and he swore. I froze in my seat, hearing the shriek of metal on metal, imagining the gouges in the beautiful black paint job, my insides turning to ice.

"Bastard…"

That asshole Blaine had cut it too tight, trying to weasel ahead on the turn, and instead had scraped us, sparks flying. He fishtailed beside us before pulling straight and flying ahead, his tires now just in front of our headlights.

"Shit!" I said.

Mr. Pierce chuckled beside me.

"You're enjoying this, Lucy?"

"Just… kill 'em, will you?"

I narrowed my eyes at the douche in front of us, noticing the black streak marring his own electric blue paint job.

Messing up a car like this should be illegal.

My breath was racing now, my body feeling like I was running a race, my muscles tense as we took the last corner, this time on the inside, sliding by Blaine. I turned in my seat, watching the angry light growing behind his eyes, and gave him the finger.

I sat back down and realized I was laughing, my stomach twirling as Mr. Pierce jammed his foot down on the accelerator for the final burst of speed before we saw who was chicken, and who'd be driving home victorious.

"How long?"

The pavement whipped by in the headlights, the darkness complete before us. And then, I saw them, the group of cars off to one side, a few yards back, cheering women in glittering dresses and sharp-looking men in everything from blazers to t-shirts whooping and hollering.

"Oh, shit…"

The Aston Martin pulled up beside us, neck and neck as we hurtled toward the end of the line. I saw it coming up, then, sharp rocks outlined just a hundred yards ahead, a gravel pit at the end of the smooth pavement.

My fingers tightened on Mr. Pierce's thigh.

"Don't worry," he said. "Trust me, Lucy."

My toes curled inside my shoes, my stomach as tight as a snare drum as we drove faster and faster. I glanced sideways and saw Blaine's eyes dart to Maxwell's still, confident face, staring straight ahead.

I covered my mouth with my hand, flinching back into my seat rest as the rocks approached, holding back the scream threatening to tear loose. And then, the Aston Martin was braking, and I could see Blaine's grimace before he pulled behind us.

Then, I did scream, certain we could ruin this beautiful car, certain Mr. Pierce had gone too far, had really fucked us over this time, but then he shifted into second and pushed the clutch. He pulled the steering wheel to the left, his other hand yanking up the hand break, and the car began to drift. I gasped, my hand tight on the door handle, pushing an invisible break with my foot, like a Driver's Ed teacher who'd finally snapped.

The car burned rubber as it whipped around, Maxwell turning into the slide now and accelerating, letting out the clutch with a calm that made me feel crazy just watching him. The Lamborghini did a full 180 before finally coasting to a halt on the runway. My breathing caught up in a rush and I sat back, panting against the leather, my lips widening into the biggest grin of my life.

I looked at Mr. Pierce, heard the shouting glee of the crowd outside, and at that moment, I knew why he did this, knew why he raced like money was nothing. He was good, *damn* good. This was his outlet, his place to shine where people knew his worth. His talent. His power…

He popped the doors and stepped outside. The man who'd called the race drove up behind him and stepped out of the car before helping his ladies out of the back. Miko and the blonde held onto his shoulders like plastic Barbie bookends, smiling at Mr. Pierce.

"Tell Blaine my truck will be here in a half-hour to collect the Martin, will you? I have a lady to drive home."

He winked at me, and I shook my head, laughing. What a crazy, beautiful piece of work he was, my dazzling Mr. Pierce.

He got back into the car and put into gear. We drove by Blaine, still hitting his steering wheel in frustration, and I smiled and waved sweetly, my hand back on my sexy boss's muscled thigh.

Isabeau

"That's right, Barry… Yes, if you could contact my associate? Yes, that would be perfect."

I hesitated, my hand on the door to the study, ready to knock, but the sound of Mr. Drake's voice stopped me short. Something was up if he was talking with the PI. Especially if he was talking to the PI without *me*.

"No, that shouldn't be a problem. We've worked together before. Yes… Very good. Thanks again."

Silence fell. I took a deep breath, then rapped on the door.

"Enter."

I pushed the door open and hung a smile on my face, before handing my husband a cup of coffee. I'd just made a fresh pot and thought of him, going over our quarterly reports on a Sunday afternoon.

He took the mug and smiled up at me, his green eyes kind. "Thank you, Isa."

I leaned over and kissed him gently.

"Were you just on the phone with the board? Because I'm almost ready to send out the earnings call invites."

"No, it was just our private detective, checking in."

"Oh?"

"Nothing new, I'm afraid," he said. He sipped his coffee and looked down at his laptop, scrolling through the reports.

Very interesting.

"Well… let me know if you do hear anything."

He looked up, meeting my gaze, his face impassive.

"I worry is all," I said.

Mr. Drake took my hand in his, rubbing his thumb over it in a way that usually made me shiver with warmth, but now sent a chill down my spine.

"I know you do, Isa. But trust me. I've got it all under control."

And that was it, wasn't it? What I was afraid of? That I did have to trust him in this, even though I suspected he'd just lied to me. Kept something back. Because Mr. Drake was the only one who could make sure my brother was safe.

And if I didn't trust him, who could I trust? Who could I ask for help?

I glanced down at his phone, wondering what secrets that phone call held, and even more so, why Mr. Drake kept them back from me. To ask for help was one thing. To be treated like a child was quite another.

I closed the door behind me and walked down the hall, the coffee mug in my hand forgotten and growing colder by the second.

Lucy

I couldn't stop laughing as we drove away, windows down, the night air whipping my hair out around me.

"Did you see the look on his face?"

Mr. Pierce grinned beside me, this powerful man suddenly looking like a boy who'd just had his first sled ride, feeling the power of the race flowing through him. Maybe I had the same look. It was exhilarating.

"Blaine always was a sore loser."

"You mean you've taken his car before?"

"His mother keeps buying them, and he keeps betting them," he said. "And, of course, losing them to me."

I shook my head, the adrenaline still coursing through me making me feel reckless. Like I could do anything.

"And how many cars have you lost?"

"None."

I glanced over at him, my eyebrow raised.

"But… I have totaled a few on those rocks. Three. Maybe four."

I groaned beside him, horrified at the thought of a super car graveyard in his backyard, full of the broken corpses of Ferraris and Bugattis.

"You're crazy."

"I fix them up, though," he said. "That's half the fun. Making them better. Bringing them back to life."

I had a sudden memory of that picture of Max and his brother, just children, building that soap box derby car with who I assumed was his father. The cold, elusive father who Mr. Pierce seemed to think regarded him as a consolation prize for his older brother, Jackson.

I leaned back against the headrest as the lights of the airstrip faded behind us.

"I get that," I said. "I worked on cars with my father and brother. Some of the happiest times of my life were spent covered in axle grease."

"I bet you look beautiful like that. I might let you help me out sometime," he said.

I still breathed hard beside him, my excitement at the thought of tinkering with those cars mingling with the wave of arousal and fear from the race still pulsing inside of me.

"But only if you promise not to wear anything *but* the grease."

I laughed and smacked his thigh.

"You wish."

But my body still reeled from the feeling of drifting on that track, light as a feather, heavy as a tank, that beautiful metal body rumbling around me. My hand inched higher.

I heard Mr. Pierce's sharp hiss of breath as I touched his groin. He was rock hard beneath his suit pants.

He pulled off the road onto a deserted country lane, nothing but darkness and cornfields on either side now, and killed the engine. Before I could say a word, his hands were in my hair, guiding me to him, his lips hot and oh-so-soft, his tongue urgent and sensual as it danced over mine.

My core throbbed, needy for him, and I undid my seatbelt and shimmied over the smooth center console until I straddled him. I felt his erection beneath me and ground against it, smiling as I remembered he'd torn my underwear away earlier today, and I was bare against him now, my wetness marking him as my own. My boss. My lover. My master…

He growled and bit my earlobe. A click from the side, and his seat fell back until we were reclining together, my eager body stretched over his, my pussy grinding on him until I thought I might explode then and there.

He reached between us, unbuckling, first his seatbelt, then his pants, pulling me closer. He kissed the globes of my breasts, falling out from my silk blouse, and then I felt him against me, his hot, throbbing tip rubbing against my folds, seeking my slick entrance.

When he slid into me, we moaned as one person, our sighs coming together, our breath mingling before fogging up the windows. His hands grazed my hardened nipples, cupping me through my clothes. I groaned and arched my back, feeling him hit me deep, before rocking against him, wanting even more.

"God, Lucy…"

His breath was hot on my neck before I felt his lips there, kissing me, holding me, tasting me. I wrapped my hands around his neck, kissing him back, suckling his earlobe until he gave my ass a smack and gripped me tight, pulling me down onto his stiffness. We rocked together, the heat between us searing, consuming, burning, until something broke, and our need spilled over into a kind of frenzy.

He wrapped both hands around my back, holding me to him so tightly I could barely breath, and thrust up inside of me, impaling me, driving his cock home so hard that I screamed. My fingernails tightened on his shirt, digging into his back, and he cried out in my ear, but didn't stop. In fact, it only seemed to encourage him.

He fucked me, pistoning in and out, holding me hostage, capturing me, making me his with each stroke, right there in his car, right there by the side of the road, beneath the twinkling stars pin-pricking the ink black sky overhead.

Tears rolled down my cheeks. It was all too intense. It wasn't intense *enough*. Rough love was what I wanted, and no matter how much Mr. Pierce gave me, my body demanded more, more, *more*. Needed more.

He bit my shoulder, and I moaned, my body clamping him as I contracted, more turned on than I thought was possible. I felt like a kiln, my core a thousand degrees, and if he didn't watch out, he might just be burned alive. But he held me and fucked me harder, sending jolts all the way through my spine with each thrust of his hips.

My thighs clenched him hard, his sexy Orion's belt clamped beneath my knees, the slit in my skirt riding high now around my hips.

Sweat trickled down between my breasts, and my body shook, my pleasure so close I could almost taste it. But I held back. I held back for him. Hell, at this point I wasn't sure I *could* orgasm without his command.

"Cum, goddamn it," he rasped in my ear. "Cum for me, my beautiful girl…"

He pulled my hair, yanking my head back as he thrust again and again. I screamed as I came, the sound reverberating in the close space as my body came apart, my nerves crackling in a burst of energy so intense, I saw little black spots behind my eyes.

My hips bucked against him, my body convulsing and squeezing. His fingers dug into my ass and he pumped into me one last time, then held me down, grinding up into me as he came, his cock twitching inside of me.

I rode him, his rod stiff inside of me, milking every last drop of pleasure from both our ragged bodies, our breathing hard and heavy. When he pulled me down to him again, it was tender, his hand guiding my chin until our lips met, our kiss soft and lingering.

I lay my head against him and let him hold me, limp in his arms, our bodies still connected, limp in the driver's seat, drops of our sweat falling onto the leather.

Finally, we broke apart, and I awkwardly climbed back into my seat, laughing when I saw him smiling next to me.

"Come on, little Lucy," he said. "Let's get home and admire my new Aston Martin, shall we?"

I shook my head, but couldn't keep from grinning as he nosed back onto the road, toward his mansion and my strange, new life. A life of drag racing and office sex and a man so intense, I wondered if I could ever do without him now that I knew what it could all be like.

He was like a drug, and even though the thought frightened me, I knew I was hooked. You couldn't just quit a man like Maxwell Pierce. One he was under your skin, he was there for keeps.

* * *

That night, I couldn't sleep. I tip toed out of my room, which I'd actually slept in tonight, and out into the hallway, padding barefoot down the lush carpeting, not wanting to wake anyone. Who knew where that cranky blonde housekeeper slept in a place this large? I was still very lost when it came to who-stayed-where-and-used-which-staircase.

But, let's face it. I didn't exactly come from Old Money, now did I?

I was lucky I knew that funny porcelain thing in the bathroom was a bidet and not a drinking fountain.

I made my way down to the kitchen, wrapping my robe tight around my waist, my phone nestled in the front pocket, just in case Mr. Pierce needed me. Something had woken me up, not quite a dream, but a sense that something was wrong, although I couldn't quite put my finger on what. It was a nagging feeling, like wondering if you've left the oven on when you're driving to work.

I made myself a hot cup of cocoa and wandered through the lower level of the mansion, feeling the hot liquid soothe me as I explored the hallways. In this part of the house, back away from the sweeping foyer, pictures lined the walls, some newer of Mr. Pierce shaking hands with who I assumed were important men —I recognized the President and almost dropped my cocoa— and some older ones; faded with time, but framed and displayed along with all the rest.

One caught my eye, and I paused, taking a sip and savoring the chocolaty goodness as I looked it over. It showed Mr. Pierce with a man who was almost his spitting image, only an inch taller and thinner through the shoulders. He was lankier, but his eyes were just as intense, his jaw just as strong.

Was this his brother, Jackson?

The two men were laughing in the photo, the older brother clapping Maxwell on the shoulder. But the thing that made me smile as I leaned forward for a better look was that they were both wearing white t-shirts and jeans, Maxwell standing in his garage next to a beat-up old Chevrolet. He looked younger, maybe even teenaged, and I wondered if this was one of the first cars he'd fixed up. Maybe even one of the first he won racing.

I traced his face with my fingernail, careful not to smudge the glass. Maxwell Pierce was like no one I'd ever met. He was so intense, so forceful, but also so reckless. Instead of wrapping his arms around the responsibility his father gave him, he ignored it, going through the motions at work while he partied and raced and hired his kinky assistants.

From the brief moments I'd seen, I knew he could be so much more. Was he afraid? Could it be possible that a man like Mr. Pierce, who'd just given me the craziest night of my life on the race track, was actually afraid to reach out and embrace his potential?

I moved on down the hallway, wondering what it would be like to have so much and yet still feel the same fear I felt—just a small town girl trying to shoulder responsibility that seemed so big it could crush you where you stood. The fear of not being good enough. Strong enough. Of not being able to fill the shoes that were left for you.

I thought of Isabeau, and frowned, hoping she wasn't too angry that I'd left her house like a thief in the night after asking for her help. Maybe I really was still a child. Ungrateful and reactive, instead of ready to embrace responsibility. I hoped to God that wasn't true…

My phone buzzed in my pocket, and I fished it out. But instead of the text from Maxwell I'd expected, a number I didn't recognize flashed on the screen. When I realized it was an Ohio number, my home state, my stomach dropped like I was going down that roller coaster once again.

I answered it with a shaking hand.

"Y-yes?"

"Is Ms. Willcox available?"

"This is she." My hand was slippery, the phone suddenly too heavy. I gripped it tighter.

"Ms. Willcox, I'm afraid we have some bad news. Your brother, Alex, is in the prison hospital." There was a pause. "He's been badly beaten."

My mug fell to the floor, spraying cocoa across the clean, white carpet.

God, I hated that I was crying right now when I wanted to be strong, but try as I might, I just couldn't hold it in. Not when talking about something as horrible as this.

"They said both his legs are broken, along with four ribs," I said.

I took a deep, hitching breath, briefly feeling like I might throw up, then steadied myself. Isabeau was deathly quiet on the other end of the line, and I knew she was waiting for the rest before reacting. Hell, maybe even waiting for me to get off the phone before she'd let herself break down.

As much as I loved her, I hated her for that.

"There was some internal bleeding... His right hand is crushed. They say maybe it was stomped on. I don't know."

There was a sigh on the other end. A horrible, rasping sigh like leaves skittering over gravel.

"Jesus."

"I know. Isa... they say he'll be okay. Eventually, you know? The breaks in his leg were set, and his hand, well, the surgery's today, and they said they feel good about it. But the worst part..." I paused, wiping tears from my face. "There was a note pinned to him."

"Pinned to his shirt?"

"No," I said. "Pinned to... him. To his skin. His shoulder. With a goddamn paperclip." I ran my hand over my face, not knowing how to say this next part, but having to anyway. "It was about the money."

"Oh my *God.*"

"It said that they're not getting paid fast enough and now someone's poking around. It said this is what happens when someone messes with Dmitry."

I cracked my knuckles, waiting to hear a gasp through the phone. Dreading it. When it didn't come, it was even worse.

"I... This wasn't your fault, Lucy."

"I know that! God, I *know* that..."

"I can get the money. I have the money. We can make contact, and then-"

"Isa, stop! I can get the money myself. At least enough to hold them off. I can't risk someone else getting involved, especially now. I just wanted to tell you about Alex."

"Lucy-"

"He's your brother, too. I couldn't just not tell you. But the note said this was because someone was sniffing around, and…"

"Lucy."

"I just can't risk it, understand?" I was crying in earnest now, my voice rough through the tears. "What if they find out I told someone else about this? I have to do this, or next time, he could die!"

"Lucy, just shut up for a second, will you?"

I jerked my head back at the sharp tone in her voice, feeling it like a slap in the face.

"I… Oh my God, I don't… Lucy, I think I was the one who got Alex hurt."

I sat, unable to understand, staring at the stitching at the edge of my bed sheet, wondering what the hell my big sister was talking about now.

When I heard her sob, the hair on the back of my neck stood on end. I'd been afraid before, but not like this. This was a whole new level. If Isabeau was crying, something was seriously fucking *bad*.

"We sent a PI after him. Oh, God, Lucy, we were just trying to help…"

My brain felt like an icicle was shoved into it, right through my tear duct. A coldness filled my mind. Not the white hot of rage I expected, but something alien. Something dark.

"You did what?"

"We hired a detective to try to find out about Dmitry, to go to the cops or maybe pay him off. I didn't know. Oh, Lucy…"

The coldness crept down my neck now, inching closer and closer to my heart. I felt a scream trapped inside of me, turning slowly into a crystal. A spike of ice working its way through my bloodstream toward my heart.

"You did this."

I heard a soft gasp, then an unmistakable sniff. The thought of her weeping now, after what she'd done filled me with disgust. The spike of ice poked at my heart, parting the soft, hot flesh and chilling me to my core.

"You fucking *bitch*. I was handling this on my own, and then you come along and almost get Alex killed, and all because you couldn't take no for an answer! I'M FIXING THIS! You stay away or next time he WILL be dead, and it will be YOUR FAULT!"

I slammed the phone down, and then remembered to press the "end" button, cutting the soft sounds of Isabeau, the strong one, weeping and calling out for me. Calling my name.

I was ice now. I was strong. And I was the only one who could help Alex, God save us all. I would do this on my own, and maybe, just maybe, save the goddamn day. I couldn't trust anyone else to do it. Not now. Not after this.

I was on my own.

"Come in."

I entered Mr. Pierce's office, my eyes feeling strangely numb after all the crying I'd done in the night. I knew I probably looked puffy and hated that fact. I needed to look good if I was going to get what I wanted. What Alex needed.

"Good morning, Sir," I said, handing him his bagel and coffee.

"Good morning, Lucy." He grinned at me with his sly grin, and I knew he was thinking very bad thoughts.

All the better. I want him in a good mood, considering what I'm about to ask.

I cleared my throat.

"Mr. Pierce? I got a phone call last night and… and I was wondering if there was any way I could get an advance on my pay. I've got a family emergency I need to attend to."

"Oh?" His brow furrowed. "What happened?"

I looked down at the floor, not sure how to ask.

For Alex. Think about who this is for. Why this is so damn important. Suck it up, Lucy, and just do it!

"My brother was in an accident. He... he was pretty badly hurt, and I really need to go see him. I know I haven't been on the job long but..."

Mr. Pierce stood up and circled the desk. He took me in his arms before I could say another word.

"What do you need?"

He pressed my head to his chest, and suddenly, I knew I would cry if he continued being so kind. I'd expected... I don't know what I'd expected, but definitely not this. A punishment in exchange, maybe, or pouting because I wanted to leave when I'd just arrived. When we'd just gotten close.

"I... I need to fly back to Ohio. And I need money for his... for his medical bills."

The lie almost stuck in my throat, but what else could I say?

"You'll have it. Just tell me how much, and I'll write you a check."

I pulled away, tears glistening on my face, unwanted, but there nonetheless. There was no stopping them, now that he was holding me. Helping me.

"If you could just advance me a month's pay, I think it will be enough for now."

"Done."

He tilted my chin up, forcing me to meet his gaze. "I'm so sorry this happened, Lucy. When do you leave?"

"Tonight, if I can."

"Make the arrangements. I'll pay for the fare, of course. Just keep me informed and come back as quickly as you're able."

"You don't have to pay for the tickets. I don't want-"

"I insist."

He leaned down and kissed my forehead, the tenderness of his action making my breath hitch in my throat. How could I lie to this man? How could I take his money when I was nothing but a liar?

But Alex needs you, Lucy. You need to do this, no matter what the cost. For him.

"I'll miss you," Mr. Pierce said. "Be safe."

"Thank you."

As I moved to the doorway, I heard Mr. Pierce dialing his phone.

"Chase? Yes, this is Max."

I froze, my hand on the doorframe and turned slowly around, my eyes wide. He was calling Chase Drake, of course, letting him know what I'd told him so he could tell Isabeau.

Why would he do that? That is my business! My family! He has no right…

But here I was, a liar, sneaking away on a plane trip paid for by Mr. Pierce. Who was I to object to him butting into my business when I was using him like this? Even if I didn't want to?

"Yes, I heard… Terrible, isn't it? Lucy's going down to… what's that?"

I wanted to run across the office and slap the phone out of his hand. Wanted to shout "No!" and stop him for just one moment from listening to his old friend filling him in on all the gory details of my problem. Because now I knew that Isa had told Mr. Drake the whole scoop and they'd betrayed us together. Betrayed Alex.

But if Mr. Pierce knew the lie, what would he think of me? If he knew this money was going to a thief and a killer, would he hate me? Would he throw me out? And what would happen to us then? What would happen to Alex if I lost this job?

I stood stock still, my legs feeling like they were glued to the floor, and all I could do was watch as Mr. Pierce's face fell and he frowned down at his desk, listening to Mr. Drake's voice slowly ruining my life.

When he looked up at me, the emotion in his eyes was like a knife to the gut. Bald hurt showed in those deep, blue eyes. It was a look that said "I thought I could trust you, Lucy. I thought you were better than this."

A look that brought my shame bubbling to the surface. A look that accused, staring right through me into the darkest corner of my mind. Into my soul.

A look that broke my heart.

Chapter Four

Lucy

"Stop right where you are, Lucy."

I was already stopped, frozen in fact, in Maxwell Pierce's doorway. He said some polite words to Mr. Drake, on the other end of the line, and hung up, staring at me the whole time, his piercing blue eyes pinning me, like a butterfly to a board. There was a pressure behind my eyes and a dryness in my throat so intense, it was almost painful.

He knew. He knew I'd lied to him. He knew that I'd been keeping secrets, and what was worse, that I was taking advantage of him. That I was using him.

He gestured to me with a crooked finger, and I took one step toward him, then another, drawn to him against my will, unable to disobey.

"Sit. Down."

The edge in his voice sent a stab of fear through me, and I sat without hesitation. I twisted my hands together, my spine tingling, waiting for what he had to say. Would he yell? Would he fire me on the spot? Worse, would he call the cops?

I saw Alex chances of survival melting like an ice cube on a summer sidewalk. Mr. Pierce's glare did not waver.

"Tell me the truth, Lucy. All of it."

"The… the truth?"

My voice sounded high to me, childish, as if I was a girl again, pouting at my grandmother's knee, in trouble for running my mouth off at school.

"All of it, right this minute. I need to hear it from you," he said. "Tell me what's really going on here."

I looked down at my clasped hands, feeling the sting of tears behind my eyes now. How to begin?

"My brother has a history of getting in trouble. He... he's very smart, but he makes bad decisions. Hangs out with bad people. After our parents died he just... he just drifted, you know?"

Mr. Pierce nodded, although I wondered if he had any clue how hard life could be for a kid like Alex. If he could empathize even if he wanted to.

"Go on."

"When we first met over dinner at Isabeau and Chase's place, I was there because I needed money. Alex was arrested for stealing cars..."

I paused, suddenly realizing where I was. In the office of the CEO of a gigantic car company, in the presence of a car lover, racer... collector. Was a car thief the equivalent of a serial killer to someone like Maxwell Pierce?

My boss' face remained impassive. I cleared my throat and continued.

"The man he was stealing for is some evil bastard named Dmitry. He says Alex still owes him the price of the car he stole, or something will happen to him... And now, because I couldn't pay fast enough, something just did."

A tear rolled down my cheek, and I swiped it away, sitting a little straighter.

"I'm sorry I didn't tell you. I didn't want you to pay for my ticket, but you wouldn't just let me *go*..."

"Lucy."

"I wanted to take care of this without getting anyone involved..."

"Lucy..."

"This isn't anyone else's battle. I needed to do this! To be strong for my family-"

"Lucy!"

I'd opened my mouth, but the words stuck in my throat at his sharp tone.

"Will you stop? Will you please listen?"

I folded my arms tightly and nodded, my lips drawn into a thin line. It was so important that he understood why I did it. I wanted to scream, waiting here, to see what he thought of me. Did he hate me?

And could I blame him if he did?

Because the truth was, as weird and stressful as life was right now, I didn't know what I'd do if suddenly this beautiful man hated me. I wanted him, yes, but what was more, I realized I *liked* him. Really, really liked him. Maybe even more than liked.

And it wasn't just the way he made me feel when he was rocking my world, it was what I saw inside of him, waiting to come out. It was the way he held me after we'd made love, the tender way he could be after being so rough. It was the balance of him that made me like him so damn much.

If he was gone from my life, I'd feel the absence like a hole in my heart.

"I'm disappointed, Lucy."

My stomach plummeted to somewhere in the region of the mailroom downstairs. He sat back, a frown on his handsome face. A piece of hair had fallen over his forehead, and I wanted more than anything to wrap it around my finger.

"I'm disappointed you didn't trust me with this earlier."

I looked at my hands again, unable to meet his gaze one second longer. I heard him get up, and then he was sitting on his desk in front of me, brushing my hair out of my face.

"Lucy, you can still go to your brother. Of course you can."

I met his eyes, his sharp blue eyes, which inexplicably crinkled at the edges now in a smile that was heartbreaking in its kindness.

"But I'm coming with you."

"Mr. Pierce..."

"I think it's about time you called me Max. At least when we're not, you know... playing."

I was taken aback by that, my protests dying on my lips.

"I'm coming with you, end of story. No argument. You need someone on your side here, Lucy. I know you want to be

Supergirl, but this situation is insane. I *will* be by your side, whether you like it or not."

He reached out and pulled me up off my feet and into a hug so fierce, the last of my strength broke. I clutched his jacket and wept against him, letting him support me, feeling low and weak but also so relieved I thought I might melt down into the carpet right then and there.

"It will be okay, Lucy." He kissed my hair, his arms strong around my back. "We're going to make it okay."

We flew together, first class, but this time Mr. Pierce didn't sleep. He sat with me, holding my hand, asking me questions about my life, my family, and I answered him as best I could.

It was an odd feeling, sitting there with him, finally opening up. It was like I'd held a secret inside for so long it had started to rot—started to blacken inside of me like a tumor—and now it had been removed, I felt like I could breathe again.

"Isabeau's done so much for both Alex and me," I said. "I couldn't take her money. I couldn't do that, not for this. And not when she's so happy. I mean, what would her husband think if a quarter mil just went missing? What if she got in trouble? What if her life got all fucked up, too? There's no reason all three of us should suffer when I can just take care of things."

Mr. Pierce squeezed my hand. "Your family is lucky to have you."

I shook my head, my jaw set in my place. "I haven't done anything. Isa's always been the one taking care of us. I just don't want to be a burden any more."

He looked at me, then, long and hard. I could feel his stare, even though I looked straight ahead, tracing the lines of the seat in front of me with my eyes.

"Lucy, you aren't a burden. And you're placing your brother's responsibility on the wrong shoulders. You didn't cause this. Alex did."

I thought of Alex, broken and bleeding in the hospital, maybe doped, or maybe in so much pain he wanted to scream. I couldn't summon any anger toward him, not when he was suffering like this. Even if what Mr. Pierce said was true.

"He's my brother."

"I understand. I'd do anything for my brother, too, even after... Well, family is special like that. But there are limits. There are limits to what any one person can do. Hell, there are limits to what they should *expect* themselves to do. You're too damn hard on yourself, Lucy. You're doing everything you can, but you can't do it all."

I was shaking my head again, but stopped when he lifted the back of my hand to his lips and pressed a kiss to my skin. I met his gaze.

"No one could."

A thousand thoughts flitted through my mind.

You could, with all your money. Chase Drake could. Isa could, now that she's rich. Someone smarter or richer or more powerful than me always could. Always, always, always.

I sighed and leaned back against the headrest, praying this would all work out, somehow, wanting to believe him, but unable to quite muster the courage.

As we checked into the prison, I felt an odd mixture of emotions bubbling up inside me. Mr. Pierce was right by my side, a fact that made me at once ashamed and grateful. It was too late to fight him, though, and I doubted I'd win even if I did. Even though this was a family matter, it was also a matter of us. He would be here for me, whether I wanted his comfort or not.

What an ass.

What a wonderful, irritating man.

I just couldn't shake him. Not when I needed him most. It was like he could read my mind, see past all my bullshit, and get right to the heart of me. How could he do that? How could he already know me like that?

Then again, how could I know him like I do? How could I know what his heart is like? What he has to offer this world?

Despite only working for him and loving with him a short while... I felt like he and I were connected. Like we were part of the same whole. It was a weird-as-hell feeling, but I couldn't help but feel comforted by it all the same.

Alex was in a private visiting room off the main corridor. When I pushed into the tiny, green-walled cell, the first thing I noticed wasn't the claustrophobic smallness of the space, or the hand-cuffs hanging from the edge of the table where my brother sat. It was the smell.

A sharp, medical smell like Iodine hit my nostrils, and I cringed, tears already threatening to fall. But when I raised my eyes, when I saw my poor brother's face, one ran down my cheek before I could stop the emotion welling up inside of me. I ran to him and hugged him as gently as I could, but willing him to feel the force of my love.

"Oh, Alex."

I kissed the top of his buzzed head, which seemed like the only place I wouldn't hurt him. His face was a mish-mash of purple and red bruising, his lips split and crackling. There were stitches on one eyebrow, and a bandage across the bottom of his jaw.

"Oh, God, Alex. I'm so sorry."

I kissed him again before he winced and gently pushed me away. Held my elbows with one good hand and one bandaged claw, looking at me with a look of pained bemusement.

"It's okay, Luc. It's okay. They say I'll be fine."

"Your hand…"

"The surgery was good, Sis. I mean, it hurts like a motherfucker, but it will heal okay."

I nodded, sucking back tears, wanting to be strong for him, even while I felt like I was shattering from the inside out, looking at him, hurt and aching in front of me, his ribs bound up like he'd just been in the boxing match of his life against a rhinoceros and lost.

A strong hand touched the small of my back, and I looked back at Mr. Pierce, standing behind me.

"Alex, this is, um… This is my boss, Mr. Pierce."

"Call me Maxwell," he said and nodded. "I won't worry about handshakes."

Alex smiled, then winced again. My heart contracted in my chest. I felt like a giant had reached inside of me and was squeezing it, milking the sadness out of me in one big burst.

"We came as soon as we heard," I said. "Alex, we'll handle this. I won't let them hurt you again."

I slid into the chair across from him and clasped my hands tight in front of me, desperate for any feeling of control, even if it was just over my own extremities. I felt sweaty in this little cell of a room, trapped with the reality of our situation. Of the danger we faced. That Alex would face alone as soon as we'd gone.

"Luc... I did this, okay? You can't always protect me."

His voice shook, and suddenly, I felt a wave of nausea rising up inside of me.

"So, what, Alex? I should just let them beat you to a pulp? I should just stand by while they k-kill you? Is that it?"

He sighed and ran his good hand over his close-cropped hair.

"I just don't want you to do anything stupid, Sis. Please, just leave it. I want you safe. This guy is not fucking around, in case you haven't noticed."

"No shit, Alex! No shit!"

Whenever I was mad, my mouth got away from me, just like my brother, and right now I was mad enough to spit nails.

"Lucy-"

"Just shut up, Alex. I love you to death, and I'd do *anything* to see you safe. Anything, okay? And there's nothing you can fucking do about it, so don't even try!"

Mr. Pierce's hand was on my shoulder, and I gripped it without thinking. Alex glanced at our intertwined hands, but said nothing. My face was wet, and I realized I was crying now in earnest, despite my best intentions.

Goddamn it, Alex. Goddamn it.

"Lucy... just, please. Please be safe. Promise me you'll be careful, whatever you do."

Alex's grey eyes pled with me, begged me to listen, to not end up like him. They reflected my sadness back at me, making me imagine if Dmitry's thugs did this to me. If they snapped my bones like twigs and broke my pride. If they hurt me in a way that made my brother cry.

"I promise."

I leaned across the table and planted a kiss on his cheek.

"Love you, bro."

"I love you, too, Luc."

On the way out, Mr. Pierce draped a long arm around my shoulder, holding me close, lending me his comfort; his strength. I leaned on him, accepting it like a flower accepted the rain. I needed it now. Needed him.

"They said he's in room 203. That should be coming up…"

I stiffened. The same voice I'd heard sobbing just last night on the phone was here in full force, coming around the corner of the prison hallway. Isabeau was here. Isabeau was here, and now I'd have to face her. I'd have to face what I yelled at her before hanging up in a state of rage.

She rounded the corner, her hair in a ponytail, bags under her eyes, looking like she'd just gotten off a red-eye. Mr. Drake was beside her, looking elegantly travel-stained as well in a cotton button up and jeans.

When she saw us, she stopped abruptly, almost spilling the coffee she held.

"Lucy. I didn't know if we'd catch you here…"

We stared at one another. A moment stretched out until I thought the air might tear from the pressure. I let out a sharp sob and the spell was broken. I fell into her arms like I was a kid again, for now, just happy to see my big sister—the only family who wasn't broken like a doll, helpless and bloody.

She held me tight, squeezing me back just as fiercely, and in that moment, I understood. She was afraid, too. And maybe, just maybe, she needed me as much as I needed her.

"Let me do this."

"No, I…"

"It's the only thing we *can* do, Lucy! What else do you suggest, huh? The cops won't do anything. Are you going to go in with guns blazing and take Dmitry out, Punisher-style?"

I frowned down at my uneaten egg salad, the café suddenly seeming smaller. Just as small as that green visiting room. Just as small as our list of options.

"I think you should trust her, Lucy," Mr. Pierce said beside me. "No one wants him to get away with it, but the important thing now is that your brother is safe."

He leaned over and pressed a kiss to my hair. I closed my eyes and breathed, my mind spinning over the one terrible option. When I opened my eyes Isa was looking at me strangely, her eyes at once wary and yet like she was accepting some inevitable truth. I looked over at my tall boss, and bit my lip. This was just how it happened with her, wasn't it? This was how she met Mr. Drake. This was how her life changed before mine.

It was so annoying that no matter how much I tried to do things on my own, Isabeau's shadow was always there. Beautiful, loving, treading the path for her little sister Lucy. Treading the path, and now leading the charge with this as well.

Saving Alex with her money.

With her new rich life, she could do anything, and here I was, just following along at her side while she did all the heavy lifting. I could never pay her back. I could never be anything but the girl who needed saving, right along with my troublemaker brother.

Would we ever grow up in her eyes? Or would she always feel like our mother? Our mentor? Our savior when we needed one?

For one moment, I imagined the pressure of having two younger siblings looking at you for support when your parents died. The responsibility of taking care of us and Grandma after Granddad passed away. The burden of being The One In Charge.

"Okay, Isa. But I'm coming, too. That's the deal. I want to make sure you have someone watching your back."

Mr. Drake came back to the table, four strong coffees in a carrier.

"We'll be there with you," Mr. Pierce said.

Chase Drake sat down next to Isabeau and shared out the travel cups.

"We don't want them to know anyone but the family knows what's going on, or things could get ugly," he said.

"I'm not letting Lucy go in front of some goddamn mobsters without-"

Chase's hand settled over Mr. Pierce's arm.

"Max, we'll both be there, but we'll have to wait out of sight. We can listen in, and make sure they both stay safe." He looked into his friend's eyes, his own face stony. "We'll protect them together."

As much as I wanted to roll my eyes at this macho posturing, I knew from the worried look on Mr. Pierce's face that he cared about me. He wanted to take care of me, as much as I wanted to take care of my family. That thought sent an odd little shiver through me.

Beneath the table, I clasped his hand in mine. He looked down at me and smiled, but it didn't reach his eyes. Fear shone there, and if I didn't know him well enough, I never would have seen it. It was there behind the layers of bravado, behind the wildness and behind the mask of his "devil may care" attitude. He cared so deeply it frightened him. Knowing that he did frightened me, too.

"How do we find him? How do we know where to meet him to hand over the money?"

"I had someone planted inside Dmitry's gang," said Mr. Drake.

Isabeau's eyebrows shot up and she gave me a pained look. I knew she was thinking about what I said last night. What I meant, when I said this was all her fault.

"He sent word that Lucy would be getting a text tonight with instructions. Alex gave Dmitry's guys your phone number," he said.

Everyone at the table looked at me.

You mean, they beat it out of him. You mean that he gave them my number when he knew someone had to pay or he'd die.

Mr. Pierce's hand squeezed mine, his warmth flowing through me at the touch.

"So then we wait," I said.

Mr. Drake nodded. "I've booked suites for us tonight at the Hilton so we can stay close. I reserved one for each of you, but, if you'd prefer…"

"One will be fine," Mr. Pierce said, and I nodded beside him.

Isabeau pressed her lips together, then smiled at me, her eyes warm, despite her obvious worry.

"Then let's get settled and wait for that text," Isabeau said.

I reached across the table and squeezed her hand, too, grateful in this moment, for two people who I knew had my back, who wanted to protect me in one of the darkest moments of my life. People who loved me.

But that was silly, wasn't it? Sure, Isabeau did, but I shouldn't think such things about Mr. Pierce, should I? He liked me, sure, but what were we doing really?

But seeing him here, flying me out, helping me any way he could, supporting me, I began to wonder. My own heart ached at the thought. Could a man like Maxwell Pierce ever love a girl like me? Small town Lucy with her screwed up family and her crazy little life?

I looked into that intense gaze of his. He smiled at me, his beautiful blue eyes sparkling.

"It's going to be okay, Lucy," he said. "I promise."

And even though I knew it was a promise no man could really make, the thought behind the promise warmed me like a candle. Even if he didn't love me, he made me feel loved.

And that was enough for now.

I turned out the bathroom light and walked into the bedroom, wearing only my white, silk robe. Mr. Pierce was on the bed, looking calm and collected, stripped down to only a pair of cotton pajama pants. I realized I'd never seen him quite like this—casual, just relaxing, instead of looking like a big cat stalking through the jungle. The black curl fell over his forehead, and I smiled, although my insides still felt like two gerbils trapped in a sack.

"Come here, little Lucy," he said.

I did as he commanded, wanting in that moment, nothing more than a bit of comfort. Tomorrow we faced Dmitry. The thought made me feel sick, but also exhilarated. Maybe, then, it would all be over. Alex would finally be safe.

When I stood in front of him, he pulled me onto his lap and held me, cradling me in his arms as if I weighed no more than a child. I rested my head on his shoulder and breathed deeply, trying to summon his strength into myself. I would rest in him now and be strong tomorrow, when my need was the greatest.

He kissed my forehead softly, and I closed my eyes, inhaling his clean scent, savoring the feel of his lips on my skin.

"What can I do for you tonight, my sweet girl?"

I looked up into those piercing blue eyes. He was so close—so very close—and his eyes were soft tonight, the startling blue holding a look that felt like a promise. He wanted to care for me. He wanted to comfort me if that's what I needed. He wanted to be here for me now.

I tilted my chin up and kissed his lips, loving the way he sighed into me. Our tongues brushed, and I ran my hand through his dark hair. It was still wet from his evening shower, and he tasted of mint. I kissed him harder, moaning now, unable to help myself, despite the knot of worry in my stomach. He was exactly what I wanted. What I needed. God, but I couldn't get enough of this man.

I felt him stir beneath me and smiled. I brushed the curl from his forehead tenderly, wondering what he wanted, too.

"Tell me, Lucy. How can I make you feel good tonight?"

I wrapped my arms around him, holding him close.

"Take me away," I said. "I want you to distract me from what we've got to do tomorrow. Please... just take me away, Master."

He gazed into my eyes, then, and for a moment, I felt like he was looking *inside* of me, trying to read my thoughts. Finally, his lips twitched into that half-grin that I loved so much.

"As you wish."

He stood, picking me up with him. I held on tight, a giddiness filling me as he held me, like it was nothing. He placed me gently on the comforter, my head resting on the luxurious pillow. He leaned over, placing an excruciatingly soft kiss on my mouth, then pulled away. I arched my back, trying to follow him, but he pressed me down with a hand on my chest.

"Lie back, little one. Lie back and close your eyes..."

I did as I was commanded, although I wanted to see him, see all of him, naked and glorious before me. I wanted to touch him, to tease him, but most of all, I wanted to obey him—to give over control and lose myself in his love tonight.

So I kept my hands at my sides and closed my eyes, trusting this man, my boss, my master. Trusting him to take me away from it all, at least for a little while.

I heard soft footsteps on the carpet, fading into the distance, then what sounded like the pull of a zipper and a whisper of cloth over cloth. The footsteps grew closer again, and I could smell the fresh scent of his aftershave, close now. I bet if I wanted to, I could lean forward and taste him, but I lay still, waiting for him to do as he pleased.

I felt something slide across my wrist, and flinched, but Mr. Pierce's lips on my cheek, then chin, then neck, made me sigh and relax again against the bedclothes. The silky cloth tightened, and he guided my arm over my head, binding me to the bedpost. I gave the tie an experimental tug, and grinned as I realized I was bound fast, although comfortably.

Mr. Pierce kissed my eyelids, and I parted my lips, willing him to kiss me, to drink deeply of me, but then he shifted, and I felt another silk tie slide around my other wrist. When that was bound fast, he slipped what felt like a sleep mask over my eyes, although they were still closed. I was a good little slave, after all. At least for him, I was.

Now, tied to the bed and blindfolded, I felt an odd sense of relief. Somewhere in the back of my mind I knew I should be frightened, wary that he could do anything to me, and there was no easy way for me to escape or even see what was coming, but the rest of me felt the tension pouring out of me as I gave up control, giving the reins over to a man I realized I trusted with my life.

I felt a tug at my waist, and bit my lip as my robe slid open, the silk caressing me as it slid off my curves, pooling on the bed. I was totally exposed now, the cool air of the room making my nipples pebble. Or was it the idea of him staring at me, taking his fill of gazing at my nude body, watching me as I lay blind and trusting before him.

The thought made me shiver.

I pressed my thighs together, suddenly shy, but unable to cover myself.

"Open your legs, beautiful Lucy…"

How was it that he always seemed to know what I was thinking?

I did as I was told, parting my thighs, sliding them across the luxurious linens. I felt more than naked, then, displayed for him, tied and unable to cover myself, open for his inspection.

A moment stretched, and I could almost see him in the blackness surrounding me, his blue eyes wandering over every inch of me, delighting in how vulnerable I was, how fragile and trusting and completely, totally his. I wanted to squirm under that terrible, beautiful scrutiny, but I lay still, my breath coming faster now, my body tingling with anticipation as he gazed upon me, saying nothing.

When he touched me, my breath hitched in my chest.

His fingers grazed the peaks of my breasts, teasing, his touch feather light. I tried to arch up, but my restraints held me where I was. I knew he was beside me and longed to reach for him, but I lay still and trusted, every nerve ending standing at attention, my senses more focused for losing my sight.

I could hear him breathing, the steady in and out rhythm just to my side, his presence palpable even in my dark world. I waited, my arousal building, knowing he was there, loving this, watching me, controlling me without even touching.

When his fingertips trailed down my lips, I gasped. His index finger dipped inside my mouth, and I suckled it greedily, wanting him so badly I ached. I felt myself growing slick and ready and ran my tongue over the pad of his finger. I heard his low chuckle before he pulled away, then trailed his finger over my bottom lip, tracing it, before dragging it lightly down my throat, making me shiver.

He dipped his fingers into the hollow of my neck before trailing downward, first between, then over my breasts again, caressing, teasing... His touch was so light, it was almost intolerable. I wanted him to pinch me to knead me, to cup me tight and take me hard, but he refused, this sweet, slow touch a torture worse than any he'd given me so far.

I mewled, turning my head from side to side and heard his low laugh again.

What an asshole.

But he was *my* asshole, at least for now.

His cruel touch drifted lower, first tracing my navel, then brushing outward, to the place where my hips met the crease of my thigh. I whimpered, wanting to push my sex up into his hand, wanting him to end this slow burn and set me ablaze, but I held still, letting him take me away—take me away on a heady current, washing me further and further away from the shore just as he promised he would.

My mind was blank except for the warm darkness he held me in, a darkness where there was nothing but his touch, nothing but the low sound of his breathing—the bass rumble of his laugh. There was nothing but he and I in this moment. No world, no time, just us. Just us and this bubble where we loved and lived and didn't look forward or back. This pocket of safety where I was totally his, and he was mine.

A place of trust. A place of heat. A place of belonging...

The mattress indented below my feet, and I knew he leaned there now, bending over me. His fingers trailed everywhere but where I wanted them most, moving downward, tickling my inner thigh until I thought I might scream. They brushed my knees, then the curves behind them, making me moan, before sliding over my calves and finally tracing the arches of my feet.

"Please... Please, Sir..."

"Shhh, little Lucy. Just feel."

I gasped as his tongue darted out, licking the sole of my foot. I'd just showered, but still it felt wrong, dirty somehow... Then, my core clenched, and I stopped caring, my mouth forming a tight "oh" when his lips closed over my little toe and suckled gently. The sensation was intense, almost painfully so, the suckling sending little jolts from my foot all the way up my leg and straight to my most private place.

I moaned when he sucked three of my toes into his mouth, his tongue moving gently between them. I could feel every movement of his mouth up and down my lower body, landing each little tickle right inside of my hot, needy pussy. My arousal leaked now, I was so fucking turned on, wetting my inner thighs.

When he moved to the other foot, I cried out, my muscles clenching and unclenching as he licked and sucked me. I never thought in a million years I'd let a man do this, but now I thought I might kill him if he stopped.

His lips slid back off my toes, and I let out a groan expressing my displeasure. But when the mattress rippled beneath me, I knew he had something else in mind, and I held still, legs spread wide for him, hardly daring to breathe.

I felt his breath, hot on my folds before his tongue touched my burning, eager flesh. I shrieked when his hands clamped down on my thighs, pushing them apart, giving him total access to my sensitive core. I imagined his eyes on my body, now glistening for him, already so hot, I thought I might explode the instant he got down to business.

"Hang in there, little Lucy. Don't you dare cum before your Master commands it…"

I groaned at his words, not from disappointment, but from arousal at the thought of his control. It consumed me, the idea of being totally, completely helpless before him. Of being captive to his will. Of even my pleasure being something that was *his*. Something he owned, just as much as he owned my body. He owned my lust. My happiness. My joy.

When his mouth came down on me, my toes curled, and I gasped. He licked me up and down, his breathing heavy against me, and I knew that he wanted this as much as I did. The thought of him loving this, loving giving me such pleasure made my heart beat harder.

"God, you taste sweet, Lucy," he said with a groan. "You taste so fucking sweet…"

He lapped at me, and my thighs trembled beneath his grip. When he suckled my clit, I threw my head back, my eyes screwed shut beneath my blindfold, tears leaking out of the corners, trying my hardest not to come apart. The sensation of him laving me, attacking me, *savoring* me, was too much to bear.

Almost.

His instruction, his command, kept me at bay, kept me strong against this sensual assault. I grabbed at the silk ties holding my wrists, using them for support as he licked and sucked, swirling his tongue around my clit, driving me to the brink, and holding me there. I felt like I was at the edge of a sea cliff, and he was there behind me, holding me by the waist, even as I leaned over, viewing the drop, watching the waves crash upon the shore, but not falling… yet.

"Please!" I said. "Please, Sir!"

I wanted him now, wanted him more than I'd ever wanted him. I *needed* him inside of me, needed him to plunge into me, to cum with me, to rock over that edge and fly with me, fly over the crashing waves until we crashed together, breaking and living and sailing and floating…

The bed shifted, and then he was there, his weight pressing onto me as he held himself over me. I felt his arms on either side of my head, felt his breath tickling my ear, and then he was pushing into me, the tip of his cock spearing me, driving my hips down into the mattress. I screamed and clenched him hard with my thighs, holding him the only way I could as he began to move.

He kissed me, then, and I opened beneath him, giving him my mouth even as I gave him my aching lips below, wanting all of him inside of me, our tongues now mimicking the movement of our bodies grinding slowly together.

He bit my lip, and I gasped, my hips bucking up to meet him. He growled then, a primal noise that made me quiver beneath him, and picked up the pace, fucking me hard, making my spine bend beneath him, my body moving to get more, more, *more* of him… more of him deeper and deeper… as deep as I could take.

I was greedy. I was a glutton for him. I wanted so much of him I would burst with it, wanted him in a way I'd never wanted anything. I growled, too, pulling against my restraints, wanting to claw at him, wanting to pull him into me, to hold him, to roll with him on the mattress and ride him like a wild animal unleashed. But the silk held tight, and he pressed down upon me, crushing me, claiming me, taming me as his hips pistoned in and out and his cock thrust into me again and again, making me ache with the sweet tension of it all.

He nibbled my earlobe, then whispered, his voice hoarse. Desperate.

"Cum, Lucy. God… cum with me, my sweet girl…"

He kissed me again, stealing my breath away as he pulled slowly out, then slammed home, making me gasp into his mouth. He thrust again, harder, then again, and I was falling over the edge, sailing in the salt air, flying over the crashing waves, roaring with the surf as my pleasure drowned me. He was there with me, crying my name as he spilled inside of me, filling me with his passion, his lust, his seed…

When I came back down to earth, the darkness was still there, covering my eyes, but then he removed it, and I blinked up at him, my dark world transformed into brightness by the sight of his gorgeous face, smiling down at me, like an angel.

"Lucy... I…"

I arched up and kissed his bottom lip, loving the feel of him, still stiff inside of me.

"Lucy… I love you."

My mouth dropped open, my heart racing in my chest again, so soon after it had started back down to normalcy.

"I love *you*," I said.

He kissed me again, and this time, my face was wet, tears of happiness and disbelief mingling on my cheeks. How could this happen now? How could I be in love when my life is in such turmoil? When Alex was in trouble and my family was falling apart?

How could such a man love me, especially now?

But when I looked into his eyes, all I saw was the truth, staring back at me, reflecting my own heart like a mirror. Maxwell Pierce was happy—as happy as only a man in love could be, and I was the cause.

He brushed his hands over my hair, smoothing it down, then undid my wrists, one by one, massaging the place where the ties had rubbed me. Then, without a word, he pulled me on top of him, holding me tight, still connected, his arms enfolding me like a dream.

We fell asleep like that, the bedside lamp still on, holding onto to one another, our heartbeats pounding together, our breath merging, our bodies entwined. I slept like the dead, and that night, I didn't dream.

* * *

"Can you hear me?"

"Loud and clear. Tell Isa to say something into hers."

"I can hear you guys just fine. Can you hear me alright?"

"Yes. We're good to go. Be safe you two…"

"We're right here in case anything goes wrong. We've got you."

Maxwell Pierce's voice in my ear made me stand a little straighter in the dark alleyway outside the garage. The neon sign was off now, but in the daylight this was Dmitry's auto body business. A light poured from the window over the door, and the sound of rough men's laughter dribbled out into the alleyway like an audible oil slick.

Isabeau stood beside me, both of us wearing microphones the size of pencil leads taped to our chests beneath draping blouses. Apparently, when you were a billionaire, you could get almost anything overnighted from your private residence. I shook my head, trying to escape the feeling of guilt welling up inside of me at the thought.

I would never be able to repay Isabeau, much less these two men who had come into our lives like forces of nature. The idea of accepting their help chafed, but Alex's life was on the line. Even if it was humiliating, I had to set my pride aside and do what was necessary.

I straightened my skirt and picked up the duffel bag full of money.

"Ready for this?"

Isabeau gave me a quick side-hug. "Ready."

She gave me a tight-lipped smile, and I smiled back, trying for once to be the reassuring one. To support her this time. I could at least do that much.

"Let's do this. The sooner we're done, the sooner we can go get drunk at the hotel bar."

Isabeau laughed. "Amen."

We set off toward that window of light, our heels clip-clopping across the pavement. I took a deep breath, suddenly wondering why the hell we were doing something this stupid. The knowledge that Mr. Drake and my Maxwell were just around the corner, ready to come to our rescue was reassuring, but not completely satisfying. After all, what if these guys had guns? We didn't bring anything with us but fists and cell phones. Unless, of course, the guys were holding out on us.

We were fucked if there was a real conflict. Luckily, this was real life and not a Jason Statham movie, so I prayed we'd be all right. After all, the dude just wanted his money. Not to massacre two women in his garage.

I hoped.

I looked at my sister, took in her wide, frightened eyes, and wondered if I looked like that to her. At the last minute, I grabbed her arm and gave her a quick kiss on the cheek.

"For Alex," I said.

She nodded, her face changing to an impassive mask. *Her game face,* I thought. *I should put mine on, too.* Did I even have one of those?

I knocked on the door, but when the raucous noise within didn't falter, I reached for the handle. Inside, men sat at folding card tables, laughing and drinking beneath hanging lights. The skeletons of half-chopped cars glinted in the corners. Cigarette smoke hung everywhere like giant, blue cobweb.

Isabeau entered after me. When the door snapped shut behind us, a few heads turned. Stubbled faces looked us over, and a few of the men muttered to one another. I noticed with some discomfort that there were at least a dozen, all wearing dark dress shirts unbuttoned enough to show their chest hair, gold chains lying across their barrel-chests like snakes on a hot rock.

"We're here to see Dmitry," I said.

To my shock, the voice that came out of my mouth was strong, even ballsy. I didn't sound like scared little Lucy right now. I was sexy, danger-loving Lucy, Mr. Pierce's Assistant and Lover.

I could do anything.

I felt a surge of confidence flow through me and hitched the duffle bag up a little higher.

"Eh," one of the men grunted, rubbing his chin. "Come on."

His accent was thick and Eastern European. He rose out of his chair and tossed his cards down on the table.

"I'm out anyway."

He gestured with a wave of his hand, and we followed, me first, Isabeau glancing to either side, but standing straight and strong behind me. Her game face was still in place like a mask. She looked like a queen who was making a regular visit to the citizens of her city. Like she was above it all. Like she owned the place.

I smiled inwardly. That's my Sis. Large and In Charge. I just hoped I was giving off the same vibe. I had a sneaking suspicion it was important in a place like this.

Men turned, watching us with barely-hidden interest, some speaking to us in Russian, others laughing, before sucking their cigarettes and turning back to the game. The whole situation gave me the creeps. I remember what Isabeau told me about Dmitry hiring cons to run his shop. You had to wonder if they were just car thieves or worse. It was the possibility of "worse" that had me on edge.

The gruff man leading us took us through a curtain into the back office. Dmitry sat there with a girl on his lap, his hand halfway up her skirt. She smacked gum and looked mildly disinterested, but he was leaning forward, his nose in the swell of her cleavage, perhaps inhaling her pungent perfume. It smelled like a Malibu Barbie I'd owned when I was six. It came with a little greasy tin of fragrance that I rubbed on my wrists once... then promptly threw away.

"Boss," the man said, and gestured toward the two of us.

Dmitry straightened up and grinned at us. At least two gold teeth caught the light of his desk lamp. He didn't remove his hand from the girl's skirt.

"Ah, just the girls I was hoping to see. Dobryy vecher, ladies," he said. "Would you like something to drink? Please, sit down."

He gestured with his other hand, and a man came out of the shadows with a bottle of vodka.

"No, thank you," said Isabeau.

"Sure," I said.

Well, I didn't want to be rude. What if it was an insult not to drink with this guy? I think I remembered that from a movie, and after the guy refused, they shot him in the face. Better to be safe than sorry. Plus, let's face it. A drink would go a long way right now.

Dmitry grinned at me again, and I found myself thinking it was almost the definition of the word *leer*, before a shot was poured, and a pickle was handed to me on a cocktail napkin.

"What's the pickle for?"

"You bite after the drinking for the, what do you call, *chaser*."

His hand snuck higher beneath the woman's skirt, and I would swear to anyone that he was touching her now, stroking her sex through her underwear. She looked like if she could get away with filing her nails or catching up on her Sudoku while he did it, she'd be all for it.

"Groovy," I said. "Thanks."

I slammed the shot and bit into the pickle. The bite was just right, and to my surprise made the shot go down smooth. I never was a hard drinker, but tonight, I thought I could make an exception.

Watch out, mini bar. If I live through this, you and I are gonna get real friendly.

Isabeau and I sat down in the moldering chairs in front of his desk. The girl on his lap blew a bubble and popped it loudly. It stuck to her lip, but she slurped it off. I wondered if it tasted like lip gloss now.

"We've got your money," Isabeau said.

The man who gave me the shot reached for the duffle bag, and I handed it over. He unzipped it and began thumbing through the bills and searching through the stacks of banded twenties.

"Looks good, boss," he said.

"So how about you give us your word that your problem with Alex is done?" I said. "Then we can get out of your hair and let you enjoy the rest of your evening."

Dmitry laughed, a phlegmy sound that ended in an epic coughing fit. He fished his hand out of the girls' panties long enough to grab a silk handkerchief out of his pocket and hack into it. My stomach turned at the sound, but I breathed deeply, and focused on the sensation of the vodka warming me from within.

It will all be over in a second, Lucy. Then we can go home and forget any of this crazy shit ever happened.

Dmitry cleared his throat, then laughed again.

"You funny girls, you think we're good with only what is owed?"

Isabeau and I exchanged a glance.

"Be careful." Maxwell's voice in my ear was a comforting buzz.

"I am thinking, since the payment was late, that you are owing interest."

"What kind of interest?"

Isabeau's brow furrowed, and I resisted the urge to clasp her hand.

"Oh, let me think," he said, scratching his chin.

The girl on his lap sighed and farted softly.

"Fifty percent for my troubles is more than fair. Don't you think, Georgie?"

The man in the corner nodded solemnly. I scowled at him. My blood was starting to heat, my anger bubbling inside of me like a witch's brew. *Fifty fucking percent??* I couldn't ask Isabeau for another $125,000. I just couldn't. No way, Jose. No way, no how.

"That's criminal," Isabeau said.

Dmitry cackled now. I mean, really got going like he'd just heard the best joke of his life, before another coughing fit wracked him. The girl on his lap took a cigarette out of her bra, and Georgie lit it for her. I wondered if it tasted like boob sweat.

"Well, Alex is always causing the trouble for me. First, I have to incur expense to be training him, then he is caught, jailed, and there is me covering up. Cleaning up his mess, you know? That's no cheap."

"You've got to be kidding me," I said. I stood up now. "We paid you the value of the car, didn't we? Just let it go, okay? Don't be a dick about it!"

I heard Max's laugh in my ear, but then Chase Drake whispered, "Just agree and get out of there, Isa."

"Dick? You call Dmitry a dick for taking what is fair? What is owed?"

The mob boss stood abruptly, sending the girl on his lap stumbling. Dmitry smacked her on the butt.

"Get lost."

The girl looked at us darkly and left, a cloud of blue smoke trailing behind her.

"She didn't mean it like that," Isabeau said. "We'll pay. But you need to give us some time."

"You got cash quick, didn't you? You can pay what is owed now quick, or your brother may have the troubles, you know? He may have a bad time."

My hand clenched into a fist, and I stood up, knocking my shot glass over on the desk.

"We'll get you your goddamn money, okay? But we'll need at least a month to get it."

"You've got one week," he said, smiling like a bullfrog who just caught a fly. "Unless, of course, you'd be more friendly to, how do you say, *working it off?*"

He eyed Isa up and down, his eyes lingering on her legs before giving me a sweep that left me needing a shower.

"One week," I agreed. "Come on, Isabeau."

She rose beside me, looking at Dmitry like she would a moldy sandwich she found under the couch.

"Gladly."

We turned and left, pushing through the curtain and making our way back through the crowd of his smoking, laughing cronies. When we finally made it out of the front door, the cool night air was like the kiss of a lover.

We rounded the corner and saw Chase and Maxwell getting out of the rented Mercedes.

"Thank God," Chase said and embraced my sister.

He held her tight and whispered in her ear. She clutched him tight.

Mr. Pierce took my hand and pulled me close as well. The circle of his arms was a comfort like nothing else, and when he kissed me, I felt the stink of the whole situation fading away. We'd make it through. Somehow.

"Let's go before anyone follows us," Mr. Drake said.

We all agreed, and peeled out of the dark alley back toward the lights and safety of the hotel.

Maxwell and I sat on our bed, drinking the bottle of wine we'd ordered with room service, thinking of what to do next. We'd all agreed to meet up after a good night's sleep and discuss options, but neither one of us could sleep. Not after a meeting like that.

"He'll just keep asking for money, you know," Mr. Pierce said. "They always do once they know you can get it."

I grunted and punched the coverlet. "I was so stupid. I thought if I paid him off gradually, he'd just... I don't know! Go away, like a... like a payday loan or something."

I downed my wine and shook my head, tears threatening me again. God, I was so sick of crying, I could just puke.

"Well, now that he's shown himself for what he is-"

"An asshole!"

Mr. Pierce chuckled. "Yes, now that he's shown himself to be a complete asshole, we have to start thinking differently. You said Chase couldn't find any dirt on him at all?"

"No, his detective came up with jack squat. And then Alex paid the price for them snooping around. We can't risk something like that again."

Max took a healthy swallow of wine and stared toward the window, his eyes far away.

"I think I know what might tempt a man like Dmitry..."

"Besides hookers and vodka?"

"Definitely."

He stood, and walked over to his pants, draped over one of the chairs. He pulled out his wallet, and took out a photo. I hopped up and peered over his shoulder. It was a copy of the picture I'd seen in his hallway back home—him and his brother standing over an old Chevrolet.

"Before Jackson decided to run for office... hell, before he ever went to law school, we used to race together. We only had trouble once... but it was enough. From someone like Dmitry."

I glanced at the photo. He looked so happy then, standing next to his brother.

"He lost his slip to Jackson, but couldn't let it go. He was humiliated in front of his crew, he said."

"What happened?"

"He beat on Jackson pretty good before I could get to them. There were three of them—him and two of his friends, just kicking him once they got him on the ground. I think he still has a scar from that day," he said.

I looked down at Jackson's smiling face, at his arm clapping his brother on the back. He knew what it was like. What it was like to have a brother hurt by bad people... but at least he was able to stop it. He was able to save him, alone.

"The only thing that would get him to lay down his grudge was offering to race again. I put up a car twice the value of his— my first Ferrari—and he couldn't resist the bet."

He turned to me and put his hands on my shoulders, still clutching the photo. His deep blue eyes burned into mine.

"That's what we've got to do, Lucy. We've got to play to his greed. He steals cars, right? I'd bet you a grand that his crew races. People like that all do. It's all the same crowd—the chop shops and the serious racers."

"I... what are you saying?"

"We've got to offer to race him, Lucy, with a car that blows that $125,000 out of the water. I can do it. I'll just need to make some calls to get my Lamborghini down here..."

"No!"

He recoiled at my shout like I'd slapped him in the face.

"You can't, Max," I said. "You can't give up your car. It's worth a fortune... God, this is all my fault! If I could have just taken care of this myself-"

"Lucy," he said. He gripped me tighter, shaking me a little until my eyes focused on his again. "You can't expect to do this without help. This is beyond anything you can handle."

"How do you know what I can handle?" I shouted.

"Lucy, as strong as you are, you know you need this. You need a new plan to save your brother, or your family's up shit creek, understand?"

I wanted to punch him. I wanted to rage and fight and go back to that bar and kick Dmitry square in his creepy ass balls.

But I settled for letting out an exasperated wail and knotting my fists until I felt my bones creak.

"Fuck!"

He held me, then, held me even as I struggled in his arms, wanting to push against something, wanting to push against this whole terrible situation, at the inevitability of me taking this wonderful man's money, yet again, when I wanted to do anything but.

"It's not fair. You didn't ask for this," I cried against his chest. My muffled voice made it sound more like *oo di-it ah for dif,* but he got the gist.

"Oh, Lucy." He held me tighter, letting me cry against him. "My sweet girl."

He kissed my hair, his strength supporting me.

"I hate this," I said, looking up. "I hate that you are so kind to me, and now I'm just taking and taking and taking, all for family drama that isn't even yours… and I can't ever pay you back."

I gave a hiccupping sob at that last thought. "No matter what I do, I can't ever buy you another Lamborghini, Max. I just… I don't know what to do."

"I know that, and it doesn't matter."

"It doesn't matter to you, maybe!"

"It doesn't matter because I take care of the people I love, Lucy."

I stopped, wiping my face, my shame coating me like a blanket. Mr. Pierce put his wine glass down and took mine away, setting them on the side table. He leaned back and pulled me on top of him again on the bed, and I went without struggle, wanting his warmth, his comfort.

He tugged his robe open and yanked the tie on mine until we were naked together, our body heat mingling between us. He kissed me softly, and I buried my fingers in his hair, loving how solid he felt beneath my small body.

"Will you let me help you?"

I looked down for a moment, then met his eyes. "Do I have a choice?"

"Why do you have such a problem with this?"

"Because someone's always helping me, and I hate it."

I rested my forehead on his cheek, and he held me tight.

"What's so bad about that? Someone's always helping me. Someone's always helping everyone."

I scoffed. "Yeah, right. Billionaire playboys need help like I need a hole in the head."

There was a moment of silence, then he spoke.

"I've never told anyone this, so don't go repeating it."

"Okay…"

"Last year, I got lost, and I couldn't find my way back without calling for help on my cell phone."

"Got lost? How could you get lost?"

"It was in the parking garage of the shopping mall. It was the one day I'd ever driven myself there, I'd forgotten to get a gift for my driver's birthday, and I forgot where I parked the car. I wandered in that goddamn parking garage for over an hour. I wandered until my feet felt like they'd fall off, and my bladder was so full I actually considered pissing in a stairwell."

I stifled a giggle, and felt him smile beside me.

"I had to call information to get the line to mall security. It was the most embarrassing day of my life."

"Holy crap," I said.

"I *know*. And now I have a question for you, Lucy. Have you ever gotten lost in a mall parking garage?"

I thought back, before biting back a smile. "No, I can't say that I have."

"And why not?"

"Because I know enough to remember the letter and number where I parked. Everyone knows that."

"Well, apparently billionaire playboys, as you put it, don't know that when everyone else does. No matter what your advantage in life, occasionally you have to just suck it up and ask for help. It's just good to have it when you need it. It doesn't mean you're weak. It just means you live on planet Earth with the rest of us."

I did laugh, then. "When you put it like that, maybe I can stomach it. But I still hate that I'm asking you this. I mean… your *car*. You love that car…"

"Yeah," he said. "But here's the thing… I don't think it will be too much of a burden."

He slipped my robe off my back and ran his hands down my body, stopping to cup and knead my ass. I sighed against him, my body tingling at his touch.

"Oh? And why's that?"

He ground against me, and I felt that he was hard, his erection pressing into my thigh. I reached between us and stroked him, loving that he was here with me, that he was mine to touch as I pleased.

"Because, little Lucy. I never lose. I thought you'd realize that by now."

He flipped me over in one quick motion, and I screeched in surprise, laughing.

"Silly me. How could I forget?"

"See that it doesn't happen again."

He kissed me again, harder, and I sighed against him. When he entered me, I held him tight, savoring this man making love to me, this man helping my family, this man giving himself to me even as I gave myself to him.

As we cried out together, I thought, maybe everything will be okay. Maybe it will all turn out okay after all.

But later, as my Mr. Pierce breathed deeply beside me in the darkness, the sight of Alex's bruised and bandaged face floated in my mind's eye. What if something went wrong? What if Mr. Pierce didn't win? Or worse, what if Dmitry took our offer as an insult? What if he hurt this man sleeping peacefully next to me, and I could do nothing to stop it?

I rolled over and snuggled up against him, holding on to him while I could, worry coiling inside of me like a snake. Sleep did not come that hour, or the next, but I held Mr. Pierce all the same, waiting for dawn.

Chapter Five

Isabeau

I paused outside the study door again, listening to Mr. Drake's conversation like a spy in my own home, hating myself for skulking around like this, but unable to stop.

"Still nothing? Well what *is* in your jurisdiction?"

I heard him sigh and then a *thump* like a fist hitting his wooden desk.

"I know. Yes. I understand, but we're simply running out of time here…"

Who was he talking to? Was it the P.I. again? And if so, what was this about jurisdiction? It didn't make sense. However, two things were clear: my husband was keeping secrets from me, and I was damn sure going to find out why.

When his voice grew silent, I waited, breathing deeply behind the door, not wanting to burst in too soon and tip him off that I'd been listening. After the space of several heartbeats, I rapped on the door.

"Enter."

I pushed open the door with my hip, carrying two mugs of steaming coffee. He smiled at me, but something in his face seemed drawn. He looked tired as if he hadn't had a good night's sleep in several days. I smoothed a hand over my hair, wondering if I looked the same way. Perhaps exhaustion showed in the bags under my eyes, too. Small wonder if it did, with my brother in trouble and my sister hating me for interfering.

"Morning," I said.

I kissed his lips and set his coffee in front of him, grazing his hand as I pulled away.

"Good morning, my love," he said. "Thank you. I was desperate for caffeine."

He sipped the coffee and hissed as he burned his tongue.

"Any news from Barry?"

"Hmm?" Mr. Drake looked up, eying me innocently.

"I thought I heard you on the phone when I was walking up," I said, and blew on my coffee.

I sipped it carefully. It was rich and bold, just the way I wanted it this morning. After the shock of Dmitry's demand last night, I needed something with a kick just to keep me going.

Another $125,000… What the hell are we going to do now? Keep paying the bastard forever?

My mind flashed to an image of Alex's bruised, stitched face, and I frowned.

For a brief moment, I hated him. Hated that he'd gotten himself into such a mess, and forced us to be a part of it. Forced us because we love him, and couldn't stand to see him suffer, or worse, die, because of his mistakes.

But here we were. Trapped, all because of one young man's screw up.

A wave of guilt crashed over me, and I sipped faster, wincing as the coffee burned my mouth as well.

"Oh, that," Mr. Drake said. "That was another associate of mine. Nothing to worry about."

He smiled at me again in that winning way he had, and for now, I knew the discussion was closed unless I wanted to fight it out with him here and now. Unless I was willing to tell him I'd overheard and knew he was keeping secrets.

I took a deep breath and sank into a wingback by the fire. Now was not the time. Not when I needed his help more than ever.

Oh, Alex. Why did you have to go and get yourself into such a jam?

And why now, did Lucy have to get involved? It was bad enough worrying yourself sick over one sibling. Two was almost past my limit.

I ran my hands over my face and tried to breathe deeply, willing away the panic welling up inside of me.

Lucy

"Are you ready to face him again?"

I looked up into Mr. Pierce's bright blue gaze. "Are *you* ready? This is pretty goddamn crazy, if you ask me."

"Well, good thing I didn't ask you," he said, grinning. "Seriously, though, this will work. A man like Dmitry doesn't just chop luxury cars. He covets them. If he's not in the racing underworld here, I'll eat my keys."

"Please... please don't," I said, imagining his diamond-encrusted keychain working its way down his gullet. "I trust you."

And the truth was, I did. Even as we stood in front of Dmitry's auto body shop in the harsh morning light, I felt anxious, but not terrified like I knew I should be. Mr. Pierce was by my side, and what's more, he had a plan to make this whole thing go away.

At least, in theory.

Now all we needed were two sets of big, brass balls to go put it all in motion.

Max reached his hand out, and I clasped it. He squeezed it hard, and I nodded.

"Let's do this."

When we pushed our way through the door, the garage might as well have been a different place compared to last night. The sound of air tools blasting met my ears, and the card tables were gone, replaced by cars on lifts, men in coveralls walking by, rolling tires, and the sparks of circular saws flashing against chrome.

We walked over to the grubby little counter to the left of the door and waited patiently for the man behind it to finish his phone call. When Mr. Pierce finally cleared his throat, the man rolled his eyes and hung up.

"Yeah?"

"We're here to see Dmitry," I said.

The man squinted at me for a long moment, his beady eyes shining, before his eyebrows shot up. He must have been one of the men shrouded in cigarette smoke last night because he definitely recognized me.

He ran a hand across his chin thoughtfully, then nodded, waving at us to follow him. Once again, we were led through the shop to the office in the back, separated from the front garage by heavy curtains. But this time, instead of drinking with a woman on his lap, Dmitry was leaning back, an ice mask over his eyes.

"Is my Bloody Mary, Bruno?"

"Sorry to disturb you, Dmitry. These people are here to see you. It's the redhead…"

With a groan, Dmitry sat up and pushed the mask up into his greasy hair.

"Back so soon? Did you miss seeing at this handsome face?"

He grinned, then winced and ran a sausage-fingered hand over his forehead.

"My friend and I have a proposal for you," I said.

"Oh? Do you have already the money, girl? Because if it's not so, I'm disappointing you bring a man to threaten me."

I clenched my hand into a fist, but kept my mouth shut. I looked at Max for support.

"Here's the deal," he said. "I'm not here to make threats. I'm here to tell you the women can—and will—get the money, if that's what you want. But, I have something better. Something I think you'd enjoy much, much more than *just* a pile of cash."

He looked Dmitry in the eyes and grinned, as if they were sharing a secret.

"What would you say to a race?"

Dmitry laughed, then coughed, clutching his head as he did so. When he managed to breathe normally again, he squinted up at us.

"Race? What kind of offer is race?"

But even I could see the edge of a grin growing on his thick face. We'd definitely gotten his attention.

"I'll put down my Lamborghini," he began, slapping down a photo of his gorgeous ride down on Dmitry's desk, "in a bet that

I'll win a race against your best driver. If I do, Alex's debt is gone, and you never bother his family again."

Dmitry leaned forward, his hands tenting together. "And if you lose? Which you will?"

"You get the car. We both know it's worth twice what you asked Lucy and Isabeau for. So how about it? Are you up for a friendly wager?"

A heavy silence fell in the office, punctuated occasionally by the whir of auto body work from the main room. Dmitry scratched his chin and gave the picture a good, long look before giving Maxwell Pierce the same treatment. After a long moment, he nodded, then winced again and lowered the ice pack back onto his forehead.

"If we do this, we race on my track. My say so."

"Done," Mr. Pierce said.

"You may look over track, of course, but then we race my way. My rules."

"And what would those be?"

He gave a raspy chuckle.

"You no worry. Just usual-type rules. No damaging other cars. No nitro. Just driving and seeing who be the faster driver. I like for keep things clean."

I resisted sneering at this.

Clean? Like when you had your thugs almost beat my brother to death?

If we didn't need him to agree to this crazy race, I'd plant my foot so far up his ass, he'd taste Jimmy Choo.

"Agreed."

"I'll have one of my guys show you track today, if you are wanting."

"And after that, we race in one week," Mr. Pierce said. "I need time to get my car here."

Dmitry nodded, grinning now, and rubbing his chin like the greedy little goblin he was.

"Is good. Bruno!"

The man who led us to the office poked his head through the curtain.

"Boss?"

"Take the beautiful Miss Lucy and friend to track and get Vlad on the phone. We have a race to be winning."

Bruno grinned, and I noticed more than one gap where a tooth used to be.

"No prob, Boss."

And with that, we followed him through the curtains and back into the shop, Dmitry's smug, choking laughter ringing in my ears.

I hoped his hangover was a real head-splitter.

As we drove back to the airport, feeling jumpier than a long tailed cat in a room full of rockers, Mr. Pierce placed a call. A deep voice answered, booming through the car speakers.

"Pierce."

"Father, I'm sorry to call like this, but I have an emergency on my end."

"Who is this?"

A moment of silence stretched, then Max cleared his throat.

"It's Maxwell."

There was a grunt of recognition from the other end.

"What kind of emergency? This isn't one of your fool gambling debts is it?"

Mr. Pierce snuck a glance at me and gave a tiny shake of his head, before his eyes flicked back to the road.

"I need someone to mind the company for a week. I'm sorry I can't explain, but it's urgent. Is there anyone who owes us a favor?"

A sigh echoed through the phone, the disapproval so clear I could almost see it pouring out of the sound system like a black cloud.

"A week off right before the new line launches? I don't know what I expected, though, putting you in charge."

I tugged his sleeve and mouthed the word "October."

"The… the new line doesn't launch for three months, Father. We'll be fine if I take a single week off…"

The sigh again.

I pictured the silver-haired man rubbing his forehead in exasperation on the other end of the line, and shivered, suddenly feeling very, very bad for the man sitting beside me. Was this what it was like? Having a parent who didn't trust you?

No wonder he was so hesitant to get involved in the company. Any small screw up, and he'd have this man breathing down his neck faster than he could say "daddy issues."

"I'll call your brother. His campaign doesn't go into full swing for a month yet, so he'll be able to take up your slack."

"No, you don't have to-"

"Jackson will be in tomorrow morning. You're welcome."

There was a click, then silence.

After several minutes, Maxwell finally spoke.

"The one and only time I asked for help with a gambling debt, I was seventeen."

"Okay," I said.

We sat quietly together the rest of the drive, Mr. Pierce lost in thought, and me wondering what on earth to say to make it better.

The perfect words never came.

Mr. Pierce's Lamborghini purred to life, making my whole body tingle.

"I've marked the turns with pylons. The airstrip should now be pretty damn close to Dmitry's course, except, of course for elevation, but we'll just have to wing it there. You ready for the first run?"

"Wait one second…"

I rummaged through my handbag until I found what I wanted. I took out the cell he'd given me.

"Here we go. If I'm going to be your co-pilot, we're going to need some serious driving music."

He raised an eyebrow at me as I hooked up to his sound system.

"What?" I said. "You have to get your game face on! Get psyched up! Now, let's do this."

A heavy bass line thudded through the speakers and I nodded my head, settling back against the leather. This was my favorite band, Adder Stone. I got pumped up every time I listened to them. Maybe it was something about their sexy front man,

Malcolm Fletcher's deep voice pulsing through me, or maybe it was just their lyrics, perfect for eating up some pavement.

Mr. Pierce hit the gas just as the electric guitar kicked in, setting the hair on the back of my neck on end. He accelerated like a mad man, and I felt the force pressing me back into the seat.

Lighting strikes
Flashing through my red veins
Rubber smokes
Breaking free from my chains…

He hit the first turn, the car drifting around an impossibly tight corner. I shrieked, then fell into a fit of laughter as I realized we hadn't died.

"This song isn't half bad," Mr. Pierce said, grinning, before he gunned it once again. "I see what you mean about driving music…"

The beat thumped, the music flowing through me, making me feel alive and vital and something close to crazy. I felt like we could do anything, then. Not only could we save Alex, we could do whatever we wanted—solve all of our problems together. Break free from our chains as a team.

Tires squealed and white smoke billowed as he whipped around the next turn. I swayed toward him and our shoulders brushed. I let out a "whoop!" as we straightened out again, barely avoiding a fishtail.

Blood pumps
Getting me drunk on the feeling
Engine roars
Leaving my head reelii-ing

A hairpin turn was coming up, the orange pylons glowing in the distant sun like the sharp teeth of a monster's open maw, ready to claim us if we made one wrong move. Max pulled up on the e-break, steering into the turn, and we drifted, me screaming with exhilaration, and him laughing like a teenager, both of us caught up in that sick, weightless feeling, then slamming back to reality as the car righted itself, and we sped away.

When he'd parked back in front of his garage, my heart still raced, thump-thumping in my throat.

Mr. Pierce pulled me to him and kissed me deeply, stealing my breath away. My body throbbed, ready for him, wanting him.

"We're going to do this," he said. "We're going to win."

I reached between us and touched his rock hard cock.

"I believe you."

He reached for me.

The car horn blared across the back lot, startling a flock of birds from the eaves of the garage.

Mr. Pierce's phone rang, startling me out of my thoughts. He was in the shower, and I'd been going over all that happened since I first showed up on Isabeau's doorstep. The job, the contract, the spankings... then, me becoming his. Alex beaten, blaming Isa, the tears we'd shed. I was just picturing Dmitry's sweating face when my boss' phone buzzed its way across the table.

"Mr. Pierce?"

"Get that, won't you, Lucy? You're still my assistant, after all," he called through the bathroom door.

I picked it up.

"Maxwell Pierce's phone, this is Lucy. How may I help you?"

How's that for professional?

There was a moment of silence on the other end, and then a low, male voice spoke.

"Um, this is his brother. Jackson. Is... is he available?"

Holy crap! This was the Jackson, golden boy and daddy's undisputed favorite. I couldn't believe I was hearing his voice now, after all that build up. I almost wanted to hate him on principle, but that wasn't fair.

I took a deep breath, steadying myself.

"He's not available right now, but I'd be happy to take a message. I'm his assistant," I added lamely.

"Oh," he said. "Well in that case, maybe you can help me. There's a meeting with product development today, and I wanted to get up to speed beforehand. Would you happen to have the minutes from the last one?"

"Absolutely," I said.

I felt an odd little thrill at being able to actually help Mr. Pierce run the business, even if it was just bringing his temporary replacement up to speed. Even though it wasn't my company, helping him filled me with pride. When he took it back over, I'd be ready to help him all the way.

If he'd let me.

"Would you mind if I put you on hold for just a moment?"

"Not at all."

I pressed the hold button and jogged down the hallway toward my room in the other wing of the house. I heard the water turn off behind me, but I wasn't stopping. I didn't want to leave Jackson hanging, and it was quite the journey to get from one side of this house to the other.

I was out of breath when I finally got to my laptop and opened it up. I brought up the files and attached them to an email.

"Jackson? Thank you so much for holding. I had my information in another room."

"No problem. I just appreciate the help. Dad sort of stuck me with this last minute, and I'm a little out of my depth…"

Jackson sounded almost apologetic. Definitely not what I expected from Mr. Special Guy. To tell you the truth, I'd expected him to be a Grade A asshole from the way his father seemed to dote on him. I couldn't stand entitled people, but so far, Jackson was a pleasant surprise.

"I've got the minutes here from the last several weeks, if you'd like me to email them over to you. Actually, I can give you a run down right here on the big picture, if you'd like?"

"Oh, God, that would be a life saver."

He gave me his email address, and I typed it into Outlook.

"I don't know why I always say 'yes' to stuff like this. Maybe Max had the right idea playing hooky."

He chuckled warmly, but my hackles raised at his words.

"He's dealing with an emergency right now," I said. "If it weren't important, he'd be there."

"I didn't mean-"

The door opened behind me.

"Give me the phone, Lucy."

Mr. Pierce stood behind me in a robe, his wet hair dripping onto the floor, his eyes a blaze of cold fury.

I handed it over without argument.

"What do you want, Jax?"

I could just make out Jackson's words through the phone speaker.

"…just wanted the notes…"

"Then why the hell was Lucy justifying what I just told Father? We don't answer to you or him."

"Don't make this about him, Max. He-"

"I know. He wanted you, but he got me instead. Happy? How about you just fuck off and let me deal with my business? I didn't ask you to cover for me."

"…od damn it, Max. Why do you do this every time?"

He hung up on his brother and threw my phone onto the bed. It bounced off the pillows and slid to the floor with a *thump*.

"Sorry you had to deal with that, Lucy," he mumbled.

He left the room, slamming the door behind him.

I sat, staring at the phone, lying on the ground, wondering what on earth I'd just witnessed. I looked down at my email ready to send, with the notes attached. Without hesitating, I hit "send."

Even if I got in trouble, I couldn't let Max let down the business. It would be like letting himself down. I just hoped I wasn't in the middle when next time the shit hit the fan between him and his brother.

Isabeau

When Mr. Drake poured his second glass of wine, I leaned across the table and covered his hand with mine. He smiled up at me, and I wondered if there would ever be a time when things like this got easier.

"I know you're not telling me something," I said. "And I know it's something about Alex. I need you to be honest with me."

He hesitated, but to his credit, it was only for a moment.

"I just want to protect you, Isa."

I sighed.

"You can't protect me from everything," I said. "Especially when this is my fight. My family."

"It's my family, too, now. I protect those close to me and the ones I love."

"We protect them, *together*, Chase. I need you to treat my like your partner. Not just at work, but here. Now."

He looked down at his dinner plate. It was his turn to sigh. Then, he met my gaze, those green eyes of his making my heart do a little flip. I'd expected anger, but all I saw looking back was a man who loved me more than he knew how to handle.

"I forget that I can't control everything sometimes," he said. "Isa... I'm sorry."

"Tell me, and I'll forgive you."

He stood and swallowed the rest of his wine, then pulled me up with him, holding me close.

"Come with me to the study, my love, and I promise to tell you everything."

I leaned into him, into his strength, his warmth.

"I know you want to protect me. I never doubted that."

He tilted my chin up and kissed me softly.

"Sometimes I forget that you don't need protecting. Come on, Mrs. Drake. Let's get you filled in on the plan."

I raised an eyebrow at that, and left the room, hand in hand, with the man I love.

What plan?

Lucy

"Should we tell Isa and Chase about the plan?"

I chewed my lip, and poked at a knot in Mr. Pierce's Persian rug with my high heel. The week was going by too quickly, time moving too fast. The race was only three days away now, the time sliding by me like scenery from the window of a speeding car.

It was too much.

"No. We want them to bring the cash in case something goes wrong. At least then we'll have a Plan B."

I nodded and chewed my thumbnail.

What if after all these days of practicing the course, Max still lost? What if Dmitry changed his mind before we could even race? What if he decided this was all too much trouble and ordered Alex killed anyway? What if…

Mr. Pierce's hand on mine stopped me as I moved to bite another nail.

"Lucy, stop. It will all be okay. We just have to get through this week, and it will all be taken care of."

One way or another. A shiver crept down my spine.

An image of Alex's bruised face appeared in my mind, and I shook it away. I didn't need to be thinking about that right now. I needed to stay calm and do what needed to be done.

I went to Mr. Pierce and let him wrap his arms around me, pulling me close to his chest. It felt so good to be held like this, to just give myself over to the sensation of being loved by him. It was all so simple in moments like these. Just his scent and the feel of his arms around me were the only things occupying my world.

A loud knock on the door made me jump, and we pulled apart. We moved to the top of the stairs just as the butler swung the door wide. A man stood on the threshold that I recognized only from photographs.

Jackson Pierce held a bottle of wine in his hand, his face turned toward his brother in a sheepish grin.

"May I come in?"

The butler looked back at his employer for instructions, looking ready to slam the door in Jackson's face even though he was family, not to mention another powerful and intimidating figure. I was impressed.

Max moved down the stairs like a storm cloud rushing over a prairie.

"What are you doing here?"

The butler's hand tightened on the door handle, but at a nod from Mr. Pierce, he backed off and disappeared into the shadows by the servants' staircase. Jackson came in, closing the door behind him, looking relieved.

He wore an expensive tailored suit, a tiny American flag pin glinting above one pocket.

I almost laughed. Typical politician—wear the flag pin at all times, even when visiting family.

"I came to apologize," he said. "And to show my sincerity, I brought booze."

He held it up, grinning, and for a moment, I noticed how similar these two men were, despite the drastic difference in their temperaments. Where Max was wild and impulsive, Jackson was calm and authoritative. He held himself like a leader even when he was humbling himself. I found myself very tempted to like him, despite his feud with his brother.

"Bordeaux. You must mean it, then," Max said, taking the bottle.

He walked toward the study, and I followed behind the two brothers, feeling a little lost. Should I introduce myself? Or wait, in case they decided to fight again? Hell, maybe I should sneak off now and try to bum a smoke off the housekeeper. Five bucks said she was listening on the servants' stairs right now.

I followed the men into the study and closed the door behind us.

"You must be Lucy," Jackson said, beaming at me. His teeth were several shades whiter than nature intended. "Pleasure to meet you. I hope I can pick your brain later, if it's alright with Max."

"The pleasure's mine," I said, shaking his hand. "I'm happy to help."

Max glared at his brother, and suddenly, I caught a flash of jealousy in his sharp, blue gaze. I jerked my hand away from Jackson's, but kept smiling. No need to be rude, after all, but there was definitely a weird energy between these two.

I learned it from YOU, Dad! a voice in my head cried, and I caught myself before I let a giggle escape. The tension in the room was unbearable.

"So…" Jackson began, sitting in a wingback by the fire. "I apologize if you thought I was stepping on your toes. Dad called me up out of the blue, and I couldn't think of a single excuse. He knows I don't have any events this week because I told Mom last time I called."

"Ah," said Max, sitting down across from him. "The jungle drums were beating."

"Exactly. I suspected it would make you uncomfortable, but… I mean, you know how he is when he knows he's got you trapped."

Mr. Pierce gestured for me to join him on the loveseat across from Jackson. I sat down, feeling awkward during this family moment. Then again, I supposed he'd been so entangled in my family drama it no longer seemed odd to him. I folded my hands folded in my lap and tried to go with the flow.

I had to admit, my curiosity burned the moment I saw that strange-but-familiar face in the doorway. As weird as this way, I was desperate to know what these brothers would say to one another now that they were in the same room.

Max ran a hand over his face.

"Jesus, do I ever."

"I mean, I'm pretty sure the place won't burn down if a Pierce isn't in the building for five consecutive work days," Jackson said.

Max laughed at that, and I saw the tension leave his shoulders. He leaned back and threw an arm over the back of the loveseat.

"So, you didn't want the company?" I said. "When your father offered it to you?"

Both men turned toward me, their brows drawn and their eyes sharp.

I gasped. I didn't mean to say that! I was thinking really, really loudly, and it just popped out.

Oh, God, they must think I'm the worst. This is none of my business! You've really stepped in it this time, Lucy.

"Well," Jackson said. "Since you asked… No."

"What do you mean 'no'?"

Max's face looked dangerous now, as if he thought his brother was rubbing salt in an old wound. Jackson looked his brother square in the eye. The earlier self-deprecating charmer was gone. The man before me was nothing but all business.

"I mean, I never once wanted to run our father's goddamn empire. He tried to force it on me... but you know me, Max. I became a D.A. so I could help the community. I never saw myself doing anything else. Running dad's company was definitely not in my plans."

He leaned back and ran his hands over his thighs, sighing.

"Besides, you always loved tinkering with cars more than I ever did. I just enjoyed spending time with my brother."

Mr. Pierce was silent for a long while. The moment stretched, taught as a bow-string, until finally, he shifted beside me.

"He never wanted me to do the job."

"Well, that's because Dad is an asshole, Max. He's always busted our chops. If it weren't for mom backing us up once in a while, I swear we'd both be in therapy."

Max laughed then, a strange sound after the previous tension.

"When did he ever bust your chops, Jax? You were always the straight-A kid. Never got your nose dirty like me."

"Trust me. Before you started school, he laid into me plenty. Hell, he did after, too, but when you weren't around. He used to bark at me 'You have to be an example, son!' A lot of fucking pressure for an eight-year-old."

Jackson's voice was bitter, his eyes far away as he stared into the fireplace, the warm light bathing his chiseled face.

"I remember crying myself to sleep thinking 'why me?' Why did I have to be perfect for *you* when he was the parent, you know? Whenever I got an A-, he'd scream so loud once the housekeeper burst into tears. I guess I just built up some armor against it, is all."

Max was frozen like a statue beside to me. I reached over and took his hand, trying to lend him some comfort.

"I didn't know."

"You couldn't have," Jackson said. "You were too young... Besides, it's all in the past."

"Is it?"

Max laughed again, but this time, there was no mirth in it.

Jackson stared at him, and I felt like both brothers were silently assessing one another, sharing a moment that was only for family. A moment of understanding and respect.

"Well, how about a drink?" Jackson said. "We can toast to the old bastard who made us what we are."

Maxwell rose and clapped his brother on the shoulder. "That sounds perfect."

For just a flash, I was reminded of the picture downstairs, of Jackson clapping his younger brother on the shoulder in just the same way. But then Jackson stood and the spell was broken.

Maxwell opened the wine and poured.

Arrangements were made, the car flown in ahead of us, and the day of the race dawned warm and clear.

My nails were stubs. I'd bitten them down over the past few days—something I hadn't done since childhood. Now, standing at the beginning of the winding private road Dmitry used as a racecourse, I took a deep breath, and tried to tamp down the panic rising inside of me.

This was it.

Win or lose.

Alex would go free, or we'd be shackled to this gangster forever, always paying, always fearing, waiting for that midnight call from the prison telling us Alex was broken and bloody again, or worse, dead.

It all came down to this moment.

I glanced over at Maxwell Pierce, standing tall beside me. It was odd to put so much trust in someone I'd only met a few weeks ago, but here we were, and I knew I trusted him with all of my being. He could do this. We *would* do this. Together.

He looked down at me and gave me a reassuring smile. He took my hand in his and squeezed it, making me sigh. How could he be so calm, so self-assured, when so much was on the line?

Cars lined the beginning of the course, gleaming in the light of the setting sun. Headlights lit the road, and people milled between the beams laughing and drinking. There were men I recognized from Dmitry's garage as well as women who looked like they fell out of a Fredericks of Hollywood catalog, walking uncertainly on their heels on the rocky shoulder.

Dmitry was in the middle of it all, lounging in a tracksuit against the side of a Hummer, laughing with his crew. He grinned when he saw us approaching.

"So this is to be my new car?"

He gestured with his chin toward the black Lamborghini, now shining in the orange glow from the few streetlights. Max had it fixed up and waxed before bringing it up, making sure we had the best bait possible for everyone's favorite money-extorting gangster.

"We'll see about that," Mr. Pierce said. "Now, how about we repeat the terms of our little wager in front of these witnesses here?"

Dmitry wagged a finger at him, smirking. "Such a smart boy, you are! Fine, let us hear the terms of the bet, Mr. Rich Man."

Maxwell Pierce strode closer to the pool of headlights. All eyes turned and a hush fell over the crowd.

"We race tonight for the freedom of Alex Willcox and the erasure of his debt. My bet is my Lamborghini Aventador."

He gestured and all eyes focused on the car. A woman sighed, and the sound of murmuring approval filled the night air.

"If I win, Alex's debt is forgiven, and he is free to leave Dmitry's service. Nothing more is owed. But if Dmitry's man wins, the car is his, paying off the remainder of Alex's debt, *also* setting him free from service. Is that correct?"

He turned to Dmitry, now swigging from a bottle of vodka like it was a Smirnoff Ice.

"Yes, is good," he said. "I am excited to ride in my new leather seats, yes? Let's get the race starting!"

A man beside him in a leather jacket signaled, and the roar of a very powerful engine filled our ears. I gasped as a candy-apple red Ferrari pulled into the light. It was a 458 Italia, and just looking at it made my veins fill with ice water. If there was any car that could outpace the Lamborghini, this was it.

I looked up at Max. He was grinning now, a wild light in his eyes almost like a madness. He was excited, intense—he was ready for the race of his life. He was chomping at the bit like a stallion at the Kentucky Derby, ready to tear past the competition and reap the glory.

"Let's *do* this," he said. His jaw clenched, energy pouring off him in waves.

"Fuck yes," I said.

He looked down at me and laughed, then grabbed me and kissed me hard.

"For luck."

I smiled and touched my lips. We'd need all the luck we could get. Despite the intimidation factor of that Ferrari, its red paint looking more like blood to me now than candy, I believed in Max so strongly, it almost hurt. We could do this. I just had to trust in him.

We got into the Lamborghini, and I trembled against the leather seats, adrenaline already coursing through my veins, making me feel like I'd downed three cups of espresso and an Adderall.

It was time to save Alex.

The doors slid shut beside me, and I breathed deeply, trying to calm my jangling nerves. Mr. Pierce's hand on my thigh was a warm comfort.

"Put the music on," he rasped.

I did as I was told, and soon the thumping beats of Adder Stone pulsed through the car, invading our senses.

I felt alive, more alive than ever before, feeling the rumbling of the engine coursing through the frame, through my seat and onto me, into me, making me part of this, part of the car, part of the race, part of this night—the most important of my life.

My brother's face floated before me, but this time, instead of seeing him bruised and broken, I saw him as I remembered him from our childhood, his strawberry blonde hair buzzed short, a grin on his face at once mischievous and so sweet it could break your heart.

Alex…

We pulled up to the starting line, and I heard Max exhale, even over the music. Felt it, maybe. Because as much as I felt aware of the car, aware of the night and the stakes, most of all, I was aware of him, beside me, a part of this as much as I was.

A part of me.

"Lucy…"

"I love you," I said, before he could speak. "Now, kill 'em… Sir."

He laughed, wild and loud. "Yes, Ma'am."

A girl stood between the cars, laughing in a metallic mini dress. She threw a beer bottle to the side of the road, and it shattered between a Mercedes SLS and a Bugatti. Men cursed and laughed, their voices cutting through the night, through our open windows, mingling with the brogue of the rock band's lead singer.

Dmitry's man grinned at us and revved his engine, flashing a diamond grill, his slick-backed hair gleaming even brighter. I leaned over Mr. Pierce and flipped him the bird. The smile slid off his face and was replaced with a grimace.

He shouted something in Russian, but Mr. Pierce just stared straight head, that strange, lopsided grin on his face, looking like he was a wolf about to run down a gazelle and rip its throat clean out. The look sent a thrill of fear down my spine. I was just glad he was on *my* side.

The girl shouted now, counting down, and Max's brow furrowed, his face sharpening into an expression of deep concentration.

"Three!"

Max revved, the engine roaring, then sliding back down into a purr.

"Two!"

I crossed myself even though I wasn't Catholic. We needed all the help we could get against that goddamn Ferrari.

"One!"

Sweat trickled down the small of my back.

"Gooooooo!"

The girl's arms chopped through the air, slicing through the night.

The pedals hit the floor, and both cars squealed away from the starting line, white smoke billowing as rubber hit the road. I swallowed a yell as we tore ahead of the other car, then evened out, driving up the mountainside. I gripped the seat with white knuckled hands, willing the car to go faster, afraid of getting my wish on this dangerous road.

Dmitry's course had all the twists and turns Mr. Pierce recreated back at the airfield, but the real deal was a winding road looping around a mountain road with a guardrail so short and flimsy I doubted it could stop a kid on a Power Wheels from tumbling over the edge. As we climbed, the engines growling, images of us crashing to our deaths filled my head.

But Dmitry had his rules—no funny business. This was a straight race with no tricks or chicken runs or damaging the other car in order to get ahead. Just speed and skill, man to man behind the wheel.

The first turn came up, looking barely wide enough for both cars to pass. I wanted to cover my eyes, but at the same time, I couldn't tear my gaze away.

Mr. Pierce let off the gas a little, sliding into the turn, the wheels kissing the gravel shoulder. He was on the outside, coming so close to the rail I lost sight of it. We were high enough now that I could see the rooftops of houses in the valley below, the lights of televisions flickering through second story windows.

Wouldn't one of those families be surprised if a Lamborghini came shrieking down the mountain side, metal screaming as we tumbled straight into their backyard and through their fragile screen doors… They'd find us smoldering in their breakfast nook, transmission fluid and blood mingling together on the new Formica…

I whimpered.

But then we drove out of the turn, pulling up beside the Ferrari, wobbling beside us. Dmitry's man hadn't punched the gas through the turn as hard as Max did.

Maybe he's scared of scratching that hot-shot paint job.

I laughed out loud, tension morphing into a sick kind of pleasure as we roared further up the tight road, neck and neck with the other car, Mr. Pierce grinning like the devil.

We came up on another corner, and I sucked in a breath, trusting the man I rode with, but still fearing the other driver. Tires squealed as Max accelerated, cutting hard in front of the other car, barely missing the Ferrari's headlights. I screeched and covered my mouth, but we made it.

Just.

Suddenly, the sound of metal shrieking filled my ears, and I really screamed. Dmitry's man had jammed hard on the steering wheel, ramming into us, the cars grinding together, sparks flying against the back of the Lamborghini. The car shuddered around us.

"Jesus!" I said.

"Fuck," Max said under his breath.

He held the wheel tight, trying to keep us from fishtailing as we took the corner tight, hugging the side of the mountain, while the Ferrari skidded around the outside, kicking rocks over the guardrail into the darkness below, barely avoiding the edge.

"I thought Dmitry said no funny stuff!"

"Someone's not playing by the rules…"

Max's voice was a low growl over the music, still filling the car with its thumping beat. I held the door-handle tight as we swept back into a straightaway, because I knew what was coming. The hairpin turn on the way back down the mountain. I pressed the invisible brake on my side of the car, my heel stamping on the floor mat.

We sped down the road, which appeared to be narrowing before my eyes. Headlights flashed in the darkness now creeping up around us as the sun dipped below the horizon. The tires gripped the road, driving straight and sure as we approached the hair-raising turn.

Max gripped my leg once, hard. I caught his gaze before he turned back, his game face falling back into place in full force. His jaw clenched, the veins standing out on his throat like cords. I just had time to notice that funny little curl falling down over his brow before the turn began.

This time, the goon in Ferrari was determined to take the inside lane. I shrieked as he rammed us again, scraping the mirror off Max's side of the car. He growled in frustration, the muscles on his forearms standing out as he wrestled to control the car. We turned hard, but now it felt almost like we were spinning.

"Hold on!"

He shifted into second and stomped on the clutch, then pulled the steering wheel into the slide, jerking the hand brake. I screamed again as we *did* spin, the sound of screeching metal all around me as the Ferrari muscled by, its back slamming into our side as we turned.

We slid around the sharpest part of the hairpin in a 360 spin. Mr. Pierce gripped the wheel again and let out the e-brake. The car wobbled for one gut-wrenching moment, but then those fat tires found purchase and we shot out straight again, the force of the acceleration making my stomach flip.

The other driver's plan backfired on him—he'd lost momentum through the turn, the friction of the collision slowing him down. We burned up the road until we drew even again, and I may or may not have shrieked a string of colorful obscenities out the window.

Okay, I so did. But I couldn't help myself.

The driver glanced over at me, eyebrows raised, and Max laughed beside me. Music pulsed all around me, making me feel invincible. Now, it was a race back down the mountain, back toward Dmitry and the finish. Back toward Alex' freedom, or his doom.

"Hit it!"

Mr. Pierce gunned it, blasting past the stunned-looking driver. I looked back and saw him swear and beat the steering wheel with his palm before hitting the gas with renewed vigor. We were only a yard ahead of him now, his dented bumper level with our engine.

We took the last turn on the inside, snaking ahead of him with a tight drift that made me whoop and holler. Mr. Pierce's grin was back, fierce and beautiful, power and confidence radiating off him in waves.

That was the moment I knew. We were going to *win* this thing. There was no doubt in his mind.

The Ferrari scraped the guardrail, trying desperately to cut us off, but we pulled ahead, now in front of him by mere inches. I could see headlights in the distance and punched the seat.

"Go! Go, Max!"

He laughed again, the warm sound mingling with the bass beat of the music and the hammering of my heart. With a burst of speed, we crossed the finish line, the Ferrari's headlight level with our rear tire.

"YEAH!"

I yelled, my voice hoarse and raw with emotion. Mr. Pierce skidded the car to a halt past the group of onlookers and smiled at me in a way that made me want to cry and laugh all at the same time.

He killed the engine and popped the doors open. The laughing and clapping of the crowd met my ears, and I grinned from ear to ear. A familiar voice shouted over the crowd, and I turned around sharply.

"Lucy! Oh, my God, are you okay?"

Isabeau ran up to me, her eyes wide with fear, Mr. Drake standing back at the edge of the crowd.

"I'm fine," I said.

Truthfully I was more than fine. I was on *fire*.

"We did it, Isa. We won!"

"What the hell are you talking about? We went to the garage with the drop and they told us you were racing…"

"We DID IT, Sis! Dmitry agreed to race for Alex's freedom, and we did it! Max won, and now everything's going to be alright, and we can all-"

"I no think is that easy."

Dmitry's sweaty face appeared out of the shadows, moving into the road and the glare of the headlights.

"Who is saying you are winning?"

Maxwell moved to my side, towering over the mob boss, his eyes like thunderclouds, crackling with electricity. He stabbed at Dmitry with a stiff finger as he spoke.

"Are you fucking blind? We won by a length!"

"I see what I see," Dmitry said, rubbing his jowls. "I see you are the *cheating*. I say no damage, but here is this."

He pointed at the Ferrari, now scraped and dented, then at the Lamborghini, side mirror dangling and right side scratched and crumpled, the metal showing beneath the paint job. Looking at the damage on these beautiful made me want to die, but I had bigger worries right now than half a million worth of damaged sports car.

"He's the cheat," I said, my voice rising. "Your guy smashed into *us*, Dmitry! And you fucking know it!"

"I am knowing no such thing, little girl," he said, shrugging casually. "I am knowing that you lost the race, and now I get the car. But, since is damaged now… I think you are also owing me money."

He grinned then, and two of his thugs moved in, flanking him and staring Max down. His hands clenched into fists, and my stomach dropped into my feet. Spots floated in front of my vision.

After all of this, we're still screwed. More screwed than ever, now that Max lost his car… and Alex is still in trouble.

This was all my fault.

I felt like I was going to be sick.

Mr. Drake stepped up beside us, draping a protective arm around Isabeau and staring Dmitry down.

"Let's be reasonable, Dmitry. You lost, fair and square. We're not paying you a single dime."

"If you don't pay what is asked, what happens to your brother, eh? What is to happen to poor little Alex?"

"You tell me," Mr. Drake said.

How could he be so calm at a time like this? He stood there like a statue, dignified. Unruffled. It was baffling. Did he have ice water in his veins or what? If he kept this up, Dmitry was going to do something we'd all regret.

"Chase-" I started, but Dmitry cut me off.

"How about instead of beatings, next time I sent you a part of your sweet Alex? How about I am giving you a hand?"

He turned to his comrades and laughed. They laughed with him, but I saw their hands moving beneath their jackets, clutching for guns or knives, or God-knows-what.

"Or how about an ear, so you listen better to Dmitry? How would you like that?"

"Fuck you!" Max shouted.

Mr. Drake raised a hand, silencing him.

"You wouldn't dare. You don't have the balls."

"Oh? I don't have big balls to do these things?"

Dmitry looked around, his arms spread as if inviting his crew to share the joke. A woman laughed and someone else broke a bottle on the pavement. Suddenly, his demeanor changed, his face warping into something mean and low. He grabbed Mr. Drake by his expensive lapel, dragging his face down to his level.

Chase Drake didn't blink.

"You piece of shit," Dmitry hissed. "Who the fuck you think you are? You think I won't do these? How about I fucking kill your pussy friend and am showing you how serious I am? How about I send to you his motherfucking *head*?"

He turned to his two goons and shouted, although they were right beside him.

"Send word to the boys inside! I'm done playing with children. Tell them if I no call it off by midnight, to finish it. Alex is dead man."

"You got it, boss," said the goon on his left.

"Is no problem," said the second one.

He turned back to us, staring wildly from face to face, his beady and glinting with malice.

"You have no more time, eh? Pay, or I no make that call in time. You understand?"

"Oh, I understand just fine," said Goon Number Two, his Russian accent gone in a flash. He held the inside of his wrist to his mouth. "Boys, move in. We got it."

Headlights burst to life in the valley, making me cover my eyes, and a helicopter whirred into the air above us. Boots pounded the pavement, and suddenly, men in black vests were everywhere, surrounding Dmitry and his men. Women scattered, shrieking and yelling, and car engines revved, but no one got very far.

"You see Dmitry," Mr. Drake said, "I always have a Plan B."

I stared as the Not-a-Goon pushed the gangster down onto the pavement and cuffed him, his knee digging into the small of Dmitry's back. As he read him his rights, I felt Max's hand on my back, and turned to see him smiling like a schoolboy.

"I've always wanted to see something like this," he said. "This is incredible."

I just stared, my senses overwhelmed as the scene unfolded around me.

A half hour later, the area was clear of bad guys, and I sat with a cup of coffee steaming in my hands next to Isabeau, perched on the hood of the ruined Ferrari. All that was left of the previous scene were broken vodka bottles, tire tracks, and some poor girl's wedge heel lying in the gravel. Max and Chase stood beside us laughing and talking with the Not-a-Goon, who turned out to be a friend of Mr. Drake's as well as a Federal Agent.

"We met during that ordeal with my old business partner," he said to Max.

"We've waited a long time to nail down Dmitry Chekov. He has a rap sheet a mile long, but was flying under the radar for a couple of years. Now we've got him for attempted murder and extortion, not to mention what I discovered when I was undercover in his chop shop. Can't thank you enough, Mr. Drake, Mrs. Drake. Folks."

He nodded at Max and I.

"Thank *you*," Mr. Pierce said, shaking the agent's hand fiercely.

I stood up and held out my hand as well.

"You saved my brother's life tonight," I said. "All three of you. Thank you so much, Agent Myers."

"Yes, well," he said, blushing as he met my eyes. "Just doing my job."

I stifled a giggle. Mr. Drake's friend looked the part of a huge enforcer--not someone I ever expected to see blush. He said his goodbyes and they pulled away, off to sort out the crowd they'd arrested tonight.

When the air quieted, I hugged Isabeau tight.

"I'm sorry I wouldn't let you help, Sis. I was being an idiot."

"Lucy, without you and Max, he never would have incriminated himself. At least not about the murder and extortion. Chase set the sting up with the P.I. when he sent his own guy in, but all Dmitry would talk with his crew about was the chop shop, which is small potatoes as far as the FBI is concerned."

"But…"

She stopped me with a kiss on the cheek.

"The race was a great idea. I just can't believe you conned Max into wagering with his favorite car." She glanced at him and smiled. "He must really care about you."

It was my turn to blush.

"Well, we got very lucky, is all. Thank you, Isa. I should have trusted you."

"I shouldn't have treated you like a kid who still needs her big sister's protection. Promise me you don't hate me?"

I laughed and threw my arms around her again, holding her tight, savoring the feel of my her comforting embrace. It felt good, knowing Alex was safe, and we'd both played our part. Well, the two of us and a couple of billionaires I could mention. I *suppose.*

"I could never hate you," I said, pulling away and wiping my eyes. "No matter what life throws at us, let's worth together, okay? I'll trust that you respect me if you trust I can handle myself."

"Deal."

She grinned at me one last time, then took Chase Drake's arm and squeezed his hand.

"Let's go home."

He nodded to us in thanks, then held his wife close as he led her back to their car, and they drove off into the night.

Max and I rode in silence for a few minutes, the Lamborghini rattling tragically every time he accelerated, but otherwise driving just fine. After a while, I spoke up.

"You were incredible tonight."

He grinned in the darkness, wolfish and so sexy, it was hard to look at him.

145

"You bring something out in me, little Lucy," he said.

I chewed my lip, thinking, it's a two way street, fella.

A month ago, I never would have imagined myself as a sexy, confident woman, ready to take on whatever came my way.

I slid my hand over his thigh, and felt his muscles flex beneath my touch. He exhaled hard, and it was my turn to grin. We were passing beside a cornfield; the landscape quiet and empty, making our way back to the city and our hotel. But we never got that far.

I inched my fingertips along his inner thigh, and with a squeal of tires, he pulled a hard right into an empty tractor road cutting through the field.

I trembled, adrenaline from the race and the bust still pulsing through my veins, my energy crackling from the thrill of triumph and relief and... something else that was entirely his fault.

The doors slid upward and cool air hit my skin.

"Get out," he growled.

I did as I was told without question, and stood in the night air, my copper curls blowing behind me, feeling free in that moment, like the birds wheeling overhead, blocking out the starlight one wing beat at a time as they soared higher and higher.

"Stand in front of the hood."

I moved to the front of the car, headlights creating columns of light disappearing into the darkness on either side of me, making me feel like I was on display—the only thing illuminated in a dark world.

He moved behind me, quick and smooth like a predator, and soon I felt his presence like a physical touch; his breath hot on my neck.

"You've been very, very bad," he said, his voice low and threatening.

I licked my lips, my body tingling all over at his words.

"How do you mean... Master?"

His breath hitched, and I smiled.

"Giving people the finger, Lucy? Swearing like a sailor? That's not behavior appropriate for my personal assistant, now is it?"

My cheeks flushed as he brushed my hair off my shoulders. He ran his fingers across my throat until they closed gently around it, showing me I was his, and no one else's.

"No, Master," I breathed.

This thumb caressed my neck, and I shivered.

"I expect more from you, little girl."

His voice was husky in my ear, and now he pressed against me, his erection stiff against my backside.

"Now, you need to be punished."

He ran his hands down my sides, tracing the gentle swell of my hips. I shivered against him.

"So you'll remember what's *expected* of you…"

He pushed me down until my palms were flat on the cool surface of the car. I moaned, ready for whatever he wanted to give me. When his palm came down on my ass, my scream echoed through the whispering corn. He hit me again, my bottom stinging from the first blow in a way that made my core heat, my panties getting wet for him beneath my thin dress.

He hiked up my skirt as if he'd read my mind, and the next blow landed on my naked cheeks, now peeking out from my lacy tanga panties. I squinted, tears stinging my eyes, moaning as his hand came down on my flesh again and again. Birds flocked out of the corn around us, startled by my low moans and the sharp *smack* of his strong palm on my ass.

Just when I thought I'd burst with need, he massaged me, kneading my stinging flesh in a way that sent tendrils of pleasure spreading through me. My nipples were hard pebbles, straining against my bra, and I realized I was so aroused, I ached, my pulse throbbing hard between my legs.

"Please…" I said, my cheek pressing against the hood.

When had I gone limp?

There was a jerk on my hip, then I heard the *riiiiip* of lace tearing away followed by the metallic hiss of a zipper opening.

"You bad girl," he whispered in my ear. "Do you want this?"

I felt the head of his erection caressing my folds, parting me, teasing me.

"Yes!"

He pulled away, and I mewled, frustrated and helpless. He smacked my ass again, and I yelped.

"Yes, *what?*"

"Yes, Master," I groaned. "Please, Master!"

It was his turn to groan. He braced himself over me, and I once again felt his stiffness pushing at my entrance. My body tingled, and my muscles gave him a little squeeze.

"You…" He shuddered. "God, Lucy, what you do to me…"

He rammed into me in one stroke, filling me to the brim. I cried out, my neck arching up off the hood, muscles straining as I pushed back onto him, bowing my back, wanting all he had to give me.

He captured my wrists and held them tightly in one hand, stretching them above my head. I was helpless to do anything but give myself to him, to open to him fully, to let him claim me as my Master, and make me his willing slave.

He pulled out slowly before thrusting into me harder, pressing my hips into the hood. His thighs pressed my own apart, his grip on my wrists as firm as steel. He had me exactly where he wanted me, and he would take what was his.

He moved faster, harder, and from the sound of his ragged breathing, I knew he'd lost his usual restraint—that he wanted me as desperately as I wanted him.

Each stroke of his hard cock inside of me made my whole body pulse with white hot friction, my pussy so wet for him now, so eager, but stuffed so full I wondered how two people could fit together so perfectly.

Like we were made for one another.

He fucked me harder, his passion unleashed, rutting me shamelessly against the hood of his car, right out in the open air, tension coiling low in my belly as my pleasure ratcheted higher and higher… my thighs shaking against his as I tried to hold back; to obey his rule not to cum without his command.

"Lucy…"

One hand moved down to my hip, gripping me with bruising strength as he took me faster. I wailed like an animal, shaking my head from side to side against the cool hood, trying my best to deny the sensations bolting through me, holding my pleasure back like lightning in a bottle.

"Cum for me… cum for me now, little Lucy," he said.

He bit my shoulder, *hard*, and I screamed, screwing my eyes shut against the onslaught as my body finally let go, my orgasm crashing over me like a tsunami, sweeping over me, drowning me in a bliss so intense that for a moment, everything else faded away except the feeling of him inside of me, and me convulsing around him. The feeling of he and I as one, him controlling my pleasure as surely as I controlled his heart.

He held my hair as he found his own release, pistoning into me once, twice, three times before slamming home, releasing his breath hard against my back. I felt him inside of me as his cock twitched, his seed filling me.

He collapsed on top of me, careful not to hurt me, and held me tight, kissing my neck, my face, my hair. I squeezed him again and again, unable to stop, tears of happiness wetting my cheeks at this feeling, this moment… this man.

When we finally pulled apart, he sat next to me on the hood and pulled me up onto his lap. He wrapped his arms around me, not wanting to let me go.

"May I ask you a favor, little Lucy?"

I looked into his eyes, now glinting in the starlight.

"Anything," I said.

"Stay with me?"

His brow wrinkled, and I realized he looked vulnerable in a way I'd never seen him before.

"I know you only took the job to help your brother… and now that he's out of harm's way, I wondered… if you'd consider staying on?"

I brushed the hair off his forehead and kissed him softly on the chin.

"You couldn't get rid of me if you tried."

I smiled up at him, and I felt him relax around me.

"Good," he said, grinning. " Very good. I'm going to need someone smart and capable to nag the shit out of me if I'm going to run my company the right way."

My mouth fell open, but I didn't dare speak just yet.

"And if she happened to be stunningly beautiful and impossible to live without, well," he said, "That, of course, would be ideal."

I grinned from ear to ear, hardly believing my ears.

"You're serious? You're going to run the company? I mean, for real?"

"Well, I can't let Father give it to Jackson. He's got his own life to live, and dreams to pursue. Besides, in case you haven't noticed, I know a thing or two about cars. You never know," he said. "I might just enjoy it."

I wrapped my hands in his hair and kissed him hard.

"You're going to crush this."

He laughed.

"Only because you'll be by my side, each and every step of the way."

I looked into his eyes, and at that moment, the intensity of my love for him hit me like a freight train.

I tackled him backward onto the hood, straddling him even as he grunted in surprise. But then, his arms were around me, and I felt him stirring beneath me. I smiled against his lips.

I knew then, without a doubt in my mind, that this was the first day of the rest of my life. This man and I would do great things together, and making love under the stars, without a worry in my heart, was only the tip of the iceberg.

I couldn't remember the last time I'd ever been this happy. And all because of one bad boy billionaire. Life was funny sometimes...

He smacked my ass, and I laughed, the sound of my voice echoing out into the night.

Bonus Material

Check out this sizzling sneak peak of TIED TO HIM: THE BILLIONAIRE'S BECK AND CALL, BOOK THREE, available now!

I couldn't believe my luck.

She was almost too perfect—everything I needed for Lisa's plan to work.

Not only was Rose Turner extremely dedicated to her cause, she was well-liked by the kids, passionate, and beautiful. Her short dark hair escaped beneath the flap of her bandana, making her look like a modern day Rosie the Riveter, her athletic body distracting in faded jeans and a tight t-shirt. Her eyes lit up when she spoke, her words simple, but her tone betraying her excitement for what she did. I could tell how much she loved this place, and when she looked out over the youth she served, she was absolutely radiant.

The public would fall head-over-heels in love with her. Which was exactly what I needed.

After the last kids were served, I carried the chafing dishes into the kitchen and got to work spraying and scrubbing. Rose wrapped up leftovers beside me and stored them in the youth center's meager fridge.

She was right—there was no danger of running out of food tonight, although from what Kathy told me on the tour, they usually had to limit portions when she wasn't available. There just weren't enough volunteers, and definitely not enough funding. Where did a working class woman like her get the money to cook for so many? Even though money had never been a problem for me, I made sure I knew how much things cost for the average household, and a meal for so many would be hard to pull off for most people once a month, much less once a week. Rose must be sacrificing her own standard of living to make this work.

From time to time as we worked, I saw her sneaking glances at me. Sizing me up. She was sharp as a tack, I could tell, and she didn't know what to make of me yet. I couldn't blame her. Politicians weren't exactly known for being trustworthy and transparent.

"Tell me, Rose," I said, toweling off the last of the serving spoons. "Where'd you learn to cook like that? Do you have a big family?"

She was quiet for a long moment, so long that I wondered if she'd heard me, but then her bright eyes met mine. For a flash, they held such deep sadness, I almost had to look away. But as quickly as the emotion came, her eyes hardened, and it was gone again. She looked away.

"Not really. I was an only child until I went into the system."

"Oh," I said. "You mean the foster system?"

"Mm hmm." She turned her back to me, scrubbing the countertops. "In some of the houses I stayed there were other kids, but I didn't really start cooking until…" She paused for a moment, her back muscles tensing. "Until later."

"Well, from the kids' reactions, you've got a real talent for it. I can't imagine planning a meal like this, much less executing it all by myself. I'd probably burn the kitchen down."

She turned to me and raised an eyebrow, but I thought I saw the hint of a smile in her eyes.

There it is. Pride in what she does. She knows she's good.

"These kids will eat anything," she said. "They're teenagers."

"Yeah, but kids are picky. They might eat it because they have to, but from the looks on their faces tonight, your food is something special. You go all out."

She did smile, then, a softness coming over her making her look delicate and feminine, despite the firm muscles I could see on her arms and the tall, fit build of her body. She was used to working hard, and it showed.

Beautiful, I thought. She really is different than other women I've met. There's something about her I can't quite put my finger on…

"Like I said earlier, I get to experiment on them is all. I find a new recipe, or I throw some stuff together at home, and I want to share it. They get enough of the regular cafeteria stuff like sandwiches and chicken nuggets, so I figure why not, right? Like Paul Prudhomme said, 'You don't need a silver fork to eat good food.' Oh…"

She stopped short, looking at me with wide eyes.

"I didn't mean-"

"It's okay," I said. I laughed at the look on her face. "I don't think being a billionaire is a protected class. Besides, I'm not offended in the least."

She looked down at her sneakers and let out a nervous laugh, then yanked her bandana down around her neck and ran her fingers roughly through her hair.

"I'm always putting my foot in my mouth. Honestly… I've never been around… someone like you before."

She looked up at me, her short hair wild and rough, and chewed her lip in a way that made my cock stir in my pants.

Whoa, there… Where did that come from?

"You make me nervous," she said.

I cleared my throat and tugged my apron strings a little looser.

"Just because I'm running for office doesn't mean I'm not a regular guy."

She crossed her arms and smirked at me now, one hip thrust sideways in a way that displayed exactly what she thought of that statement.

"Mm hmm. You're just a regular ol' billionaire who just happened to have a star career as a D.A. and are now trying to run my state. No biggie, right? Just one of the guys."

"Exactly," I said.

I chuckled at the look on her face. She was something else, indeed.

"Seriously, though, Rose… I know you can cook, and I see how much you love helping here, but how do you afford it? Is that rude to ask?"

She straightened up and stared at me, her jaw clenching for the space of a heartbeat.

"I have a job. This place is important, so I make it happen, okay? I'm good… We're good."

I licked my bottom lip, and noticed her eyes flick down to my mouth, then back up again, meeting my gaze.

"I'm not saying you're not making it happen. I'm just wondering… Would you be interested in another job? A much, *much*, better paying one than your current employment?"

"How do you know it's better paying? You don't even know what I do."

She was getting angry, and I could tell she was starting to view me as an outsider again. An intruder in her world. I had to talk fast, or I wouldn't have a chance to convince her of what I needed.

"How does five million dollars for a year of work sound?"

She raised a finger, her mouth already forming an argument, when she froze, mid-motion. Her eyes widened until I thought they might fall out, and her mouth worked, as if trying to speak, but her brain wouldn't provide the words.

It would have been funny, if my political career didn't hinge on this one moment. This one woman.

"A problem just popped up for me," I said, "and I need your help to make it go away. I probably should have asked this first, but, are you currently seeing anyone?"

That seemed to snap her out of it.

She reeled back until her butt hit the counter behind her, her eyebrow raising incredulously.

"What?"

"Well, the job would be highly unusual, and I'd need you to keep things absolutely confidential during the year you work for me. I also can't have you seeing anyone, or you won't be right for this position."

"I… What?"

"Rose, I can't tell you more details until I know you're interested. I can't disclose my problem to just anyone. I need you to sign a confidentiality agreement before I can tell you about what you'd be doing if you accept my job offer."

"But… did you say *million*?"

"Five million dollars. For one year working for me. It can all be yours, Rose, along with an unrestricted spending allowance during that year, lodging, health care—the whole enchilada. I will take excellent care of you."

I moved closer, and she didn't flinch away. I put my hands on her shoulders. This close, I could smell the soft scent of her shampoo, something fruity and sensual.

"If you take this job, Rose," I said, "You can do anything you'd like for the rest of you life with the right financial planning. You can make feeding these kids a full time job and live off the interest."

She looked up into my eyes, her breathing shallow, and I could see her trying to take this all in. What must this be like for her? A stranger offering her more money than she could ever make in a hundred years at a high-paying management job.

Life-changing money.

It was funny to think that an amount like this could simultaneously be so huge and so small, depending on who you are. I spent five million on a vacation home in Bora Bora smaller than the east wing of my estate here. I realized now I've only been there once.

I'd almost forgotten I owned it.

"What do you say? Are you willing to hear more?"

She opened her mouth, then closed it again, squeezing her eyes shut like she was harnessing her chi. She finally opened them and nodded.

"Excellent! I can have the confidentiality agreement drawn up immediately. Are you available tomorrow evening to meet?"

She nodded again, and a small squeak left her lips. I smiled and ran my hands over her shoulders.

"Good. Let me have your address, and I'll send a car for you at 7:00 p.m. We can discuss business over dinner."

I handed her my cell phone and she plugged in her information with trembling hands.

"Thank you," I said. "I appreciate you hearing me out."

I walked toward the back door, when I heard her release the breath she'd been holding.

"Wait."

I turned back. She had her hand on her hip again, her chin held high.

"Why me?"

I grinned and put my hand on the door handle.

"Because you're perfect."

I didn't wait to see her reaction, but I smiled as I stepped out into the cool, night air.

This was going to work. I could feel it.

7814641R00087

Made in the USA
San Bernardino, CA
17 January 2014